# DANCER'S LUCK

*To*
*my friend Ian S. Campbell of Sligachan,*
*with many thanks for his true Highland*
*courtesy and kindness in answering my*
*many questions in connection with this book.*

*BY THE SAME AUTHOR*
*ALSO IN ARMADA*

DANCING PEEL

*Dancer's Luck* was first published in the
U.K. in 1955 by Thomas Nelson & Sons Ltd.
This edition was published in 1965 by
May Fair Books Ltd, Dorset House,
13a Old Burlington Street, London, W.1,
and was printed in Great Britain by
Love & Malcomson Ltd, Brighton Road,
Redhill, Surrey, England.

LORNA HILL

# Dancer's Luck

COVER & TEXT
ILLUSTRATIONS BY
MARY GERNAT

ARMADA
PAPERBACKS
for Boys & Girls

The Outer Hebrides

Duntulm

Storr Old Man

Macleods Maidens    S.Macleods Table    Dunvegan Castle    PORTREE    Sligachan

S.Almadair    Dearg Sgo Ghreadaidh    Sg nan Gillean    Blaven    Clach Glas

Garsven    THE BLACK CUILLIN    Loch Coruisk    Coire Uaigneich

STRATHAIRD

Loch Scavaig    Loch Slapin

Elgol

SLEAT

Ardavasar    Armadale

THE ISLAND

OF

SKYE    MALLAIG

Sound of S

------ Roads
Route followed by Annette and Angus

*"Darling Shuna!" cried Annette.*
*"Thank you for carrying me all this way."*

# PART ONE

## Cock o' the North

HIS nickname was Cock o' the North, so it is fitting, perhaps, that we should meet him standing on the top of Clach Glas, the Matterhorn of Skye. He owed his nickname partly to the fact that he was a remote descendant of George, fifth Duke of Gordon, who was the first owner of it, and after whom the famous Highland pipe tune is named, but principally because of his renown as a climber. It was said of Jaimie Gordon that where a fly could climb, so could he! It was uncanny the way his fingers found 'holds' in a seemingly unbroken face of rock. His climbing companions admired and trusted him, and they knew that if a way to the top was possible, Jamie would find it and lead them up in safety.

I must explain that this picture of Cock o' the North is true only of Jaimie as a mountaineer. Below, as he strode over his estate, composed mostly of rough and boggy moorland dominated by a half-ruined castle and a clachan of cottages, he was just Gordon, of Airdrochnish, the laird, a quiet softly-spoken young man, who looked more like a swarthy Spaniard than the Highlander that he was. There are many young men like Jamie in the Island—men with dark eyes, black curly hair and olive complexion, heritage of the Spaniards whose galleons had been wrecked on the rocky shores of Vaternish long ago, and who had come ashore and made their homes in the Misty Isle. Jamie's dark-eyed mother (dead now) was a descendant of one of them.

It was cold on the mountain that day, but Jamie was hot from climbing. He had scrambled down the north face of Blaven, and up over the sensational ridge to the top of Clach Glas, and was now drinking in the view before descending to earth again by way of the rocky pinnacles and the easy scree slopes of Coire Uaigneich. His kilt blew round his knees, for the summer breeze had become a cutting wind on the mountain peak. One brown hand rested on his ice-axe, while the other lightly caressed the neat coil of nylon rope slung over his left shoulder, on top of his rucksack. His heavily nailed boots, worn over many pairs of thick socks, rested quietly on the deep soft moss that carpets the top of the peak.

A light cloud of mist boiled up at his feet in that unaccountable way mist has on the tops of mountains, even on the finest of days, and he waited patiently for the view to reappear. Ah, here it came! It was like being in an aeroplane and gazing down through a hole in the clouds at the earth far below. Although he was well acquainted with magnificent views, he drew in his breath at the matchless sight spread out beneath him. At his feet, nearly three thousand feet below, lay Loch Slapin, and, on its northern shore, the district called Airdrochnish, and his own small village of Airdrochan, hidden in its silver birch woods. He could see his castle, with its round turrets, standing on its bold headland, though from this height the craggy cliff looked a mere seaweedy rock. He could even see—or thought he could—the smoke issuing from its many twisted chimneys, and he smiled. He had been forced to let his castle to rich and romantic-minded Americans, and Americans believe in warmth at all times. He saw in his imagination Mamie Slaughter piling the peats in the huge old fireplaces on this lovely August evening, exclaiming the while in her nasal drawl: 'Say, folks, we gotta get this place heated up some way. It may be awful historic, but it sure is awful cold!'

Besides Mamie Slaughter, there was Pop, a mild insignificant little man, who had, in some unaccountable way, made a vast amount of dollars, and whose chief function in life was now, so it seemed, to trot round after his wife helping her to spend them. To complete the Slaughter household, there was Deborah. The whole household revolved round Deborah, spoilt and pretty. At least she would have been spoilt if it had been possible to spoil her, but fortunately it wasn't. Deborah remained just as sweet and good-natured a girl as you would meet anywhere. She was seventeen, and had just finished her last term at her Edinburgh boarding-school, where she had been sent because her mother's best friend, Miriam, had been educated in Edinburgh when a girl, and had painted such glowing pictures of Scotland and the superiority of its education that Mamie had been determined that her darling Deborah should go to school there too. After the summer vacation Deborah was to go to a 'finishing school' in Switzerland for a year, before making her curtsy to the Queen at a Scottish 'Drawing Room'. Her parents were taking her to Lausanne in September, and were now having a holiday themselves. Hence the castle.

On a grass-grown terrace which ran across the whole south front of the building, and which incidentally commanded an unsurpassed view of Blaven, sat Mamie Slaughter. On a table at her side was a large box of notepaper, highly scented and edged with tartan (of which more anon). She was writing to her friend, Miriam, who lived in far away Chicago.

*Dearest Miriam,*

*Here we are at last in our castle, and gosh, you should just see the place! No electric light, no steam-heating, no radio or television, and no iced drinks. There's a causeway full of potholes over to the castle from the shore, and a road leading to a place called Elgol full of positive mine-craters, and we break a spring every time we take a ride in the automobile. There's a small village (they call it a 'clachan') about a quarter of a mile away, with a few cottages and a post-office in one of them. No sidewalks, no candy-stores, and not a single movie-theater nearer than Fort William, and that's over on the mainland with ranges of mountains between. Our castle is perched on a place called Dun Mor, at the edge of a sea lake (they call it a 'loch' here) whose name is Slapin. It's real cute, isn't it—the loch's name, I mean!*

*You go to sleep at night listening to the waves lapping against your bedroom wall, and wake in the morning to find a seagull sitting on your windowsill making the cutest noises, and like as not you find that a cloud from the mountains across the loch has drifted in through the window, and everything is as wet as wet. And talk about lonely! There are no railroads in Skye, you know, and only a bus to Broadford—that's the nearest big village —from that place I told you about called Elgol, and*

9

then it's really run for the school children, so in the vacation you never know whether it will turn up, and it usually doesn't. It's fortunate we have the convertible, though for that matter it might just as well be a hard-top saloon because it rains every day, and most times it rains all day.

I can hear the telephone bell ringing, so I must go and answer it, because the library (where the phone is) is miles away from the kitchens and none of the servants can possibly hear it.

Later:

What d'yer know! That was Deborah and her friend, Sheena MacDonald. They're at Broadford on their way over here, and they rang up to ask me to send over the convertible to pick them up. Deborah's been spending a week at Glendounie, Sheena's home. It's in the south of the Island—the part called Sleat (only they pronounce it 'slate'), and Deborah says that Sheena is kin to the MacDonalds of Sleat, and her ancestors were Lords of the Isles. Say, don't that sound real romantic?

It's what is called the Skye Gathering here just now. That's when all the clans gather together, and a lot of other people too, and they play what they call 'Games', only they seem to me to be just real hard work—things like Tossing the Caber. That's a great tree like a tele-graph pole, and they throw it for miles. Well, perhaps that's a little exaggerated, but anyway they throw it for an awful long way. And they dance too—Highland reels, and things called strathspeys, and they're all dressed up in kilts, and plaids and bonnets. They sure look mar-vellous! Then at the end there's a Grand Ball in the Skye Gathering Hall in Portree, that's the capital of the Island, and everyone who's anyone in Skye goes to it, and a lot of other people besides from the mainland. We've made up a party for it—some people called Mac-Leod, and a young man called Iain Drummond of Glen-mor, and his sisters Flora and Elspeth, and of course Deborah and Sheena, and Jamie Gordan.

Honey, you should just see Jamie Gordon—he's the young man we've rented the castle from. He's called 'the Laird', or 'Gordon of Airdrochnish,' or 'Airdroch-

10

nish' alone, or sometimes just 'Himself'. He's the cutest thing! Black curly hair, and the saddest of dark eyes, and a dirk (they call it a 'sgian dubh') in his stocking. Yes, of course he wears the kilt. You feel he might knife you as soon as look at you, but of course he never does. In fact, he's awful polite. He has to be, poor young man (oh, yes, he's only twenty-three) because he hasn't a cent to bless himself with. In fact, it's rumoured hereabouts that he may have to sell his castle before long, or let it fall into ruin (and goodness knows it's nearly that now!), and go and earn his living on the mainland. He's a veterinary surgeon, you know. It's sad, ain't it—I mean about him having to sell the castle?

Well, honey, I think I've told you most everything, so how about you mailing me a nice long letter with all the news from back home.

With every good wish from your old friend,

Mamie.

P.S. Oh, I've just remembered the cutest story I heard this morning in the village. You know, the way these people behave on Sunday (they call it the Sabbath) seems mighty queer to us Americans. They sit around all day with the window curtains drawn, doing absolutely nothing, except when they're at the kirk (that's the church). There's no transport at all in the island on the Sabbath Day——not even the ferry, let alone a bus. They don't even think it's right to walk! Well, one Sunday a minister called Andrew Mactavish was preaching in the village. He was taking a stroll after his midday meal, and he happened to pass by old Seumas MacDonald's cottage, and there was Seumas sitting at his door looking awfu' dour (you see, I'm getting real good at the language!).

'Good day to ye, Seumas,' says the minister.

No answer.

'I am saying good day to ye,' repeats Andrew.

'I have heard ye.'

'Now I am knowing what it is ye are thinking, Seumas,' goes on the minister. 'Ye are thinking it's no the right thing for me to be taking a wee walk on the Lord's Day. Is that no what ye are thinking?'

'Aye,' says Seumas, still looking awfu' dour.

'Have ye no heard, mon,' says Andrew, 'aboot Our

11

*Lord walking through the harvest fields on the Sabbath Day?'*

*'Aye, I have that,' answers Seumas. 'And I can tell ye, Andrew, it's no the better of Him for that that I'm thinking.'*

*Now isn't that just the cutest thing you ever heard?*
*Love again, Mamie.*

At the precise moment when Mamie was writing these words on her tartan-edged notepaper, Jamie, on his peak above, was thinking about his future. Yes, he must leave Airdrochnish and seek fame and fortune elsewhere, as so many of his fellow Islanders had done before him. It wasn't that his services as a veterinary surgeon were not needed here on the Isle, but that the district was too large and far-flung for him to do his work properly, let alone to make it pay. He needed a new car (his own was dropping to pieces and always let him down at the most inopportune moments), and a motor launch, and much new and expensive equipment. He might as well cry for the moon! These things needed capital. He had tried to borrow it, but the bank wouldn't advance so much money without security, and all the security Jaimie had was a half-ruined castle, and a wild and beautiful village at the foot of Blaven which cost him more in repairs than it brought him in rents. The bank manager was sympathetic but firm. He advised the young man to leave the Island and go where his services would be well rewarded. Bank managers are not sentimentalists—they can't afford to be.

When he was old he would come back, maybe, thought Jaimie, but by that time he would no longer be able to climb to the top of this dangerous ridge and stand there, proud as an eagle or as his famous ancestor, the Cock o' the North. His eyes, a shade more sombre than usual, swept once more over the lovely prospect. The grim shattered face of Blaven, seamed and wrinkled as the skin on the neck of an ancient tortoise, made a fitting foreground for the majestic horse-shoe of the Black Cuillin* range, with its cloud-riven pinnacles and gashed skyline, curving in rocky splendour from the hook of Gars Bheinn on the south, to the graceful peak of Sgurr nan Gillian on the north. Hidden

* Pronounced 'Coolin'

in the fastnesses of these mountains lay dark and mysterious Loch Coruisk, but he could not see it from where he stood. Far below him on the north-west lay stony Glen Sligachan, the scene of wildest desolation. Its tiny lochans glinted in the heather like two dark eyes. Out in the shimmering sea lay islands with strange names—Rhum, Muck, Eigg and peaceful Canna. Still farther away, floating in the blue air like dream islands, lay the Outer Hebrides.

He looked down at Loch Slapin and his castle again, and his thoughts returned to the Slaughters. They were so guileless and forthright! To Jaimie, with his dark and stormy ancestry, his Gaelic temperament, thoughtful and silent, they were like charming children. Take their passion for tartan, for instance. They didn't keep to the one tartan, either, but blossomed out in any that took their fancy, or fitted in with their colour scheme. Bigger, Brighter and Better was the Slaughter motto in all things, and they certainly followed it out with their tartans. They wore tartans that made poor Jaimie blush. Tartan kilts, skirts, shirts and coats. Curtains, bedspreads, travelling-rugs followed suit, and even the Slaughter underwear broke out into tartan in the most unexpected places—at least, Morag MacLeod said so. Morag helped Mairi Campbell in the kitchen and did the laundry, so who should know better than she about the Mistress's chemises with the edges bound in the Macleod tartan and the Master's tartan braces? In the Gaelic, and with suitable dramatic gestures, she described also how the motor car had just come back from Fort William with tartan covers put upon it, and in the Stuart tartan, this time, because it had red in it and matched the car. 'Yes, and catched the eye', which (in the Slaughters' eyes) was even more important.

'And the Mistress's bedgoons are in the tartan too,' she told her fascinated audience. Donald Gordon, the laird's shepherd, and his six solemn-faced children. 'And made of silk, they are, and if you are wishful to know why the Mistress and the Master should be wearing the tartan of the Stuarts for their car, the tartan of the MacLeods for their underwear, and the tartan of the MacDonalds and the MacLeans for their curtains and bed-linen—why, one can only say that they are Americans,' added Morag with an expressive shrug of her shoulders. As far as she was concerned, that was that!

13

It is only fair to say that the Slaughters thought the inhabitants of Skye just as funny.

## The Lamb

JAIMIE left the mountain top as the sun began to go down. He followed the crest of the rough ridge first down the edge of a steeply tilted slab, then down a short chimney, along a narrow ledge and over broken rocks to a deep black gash. He climbed over one pinnacle, around another, and finally over easy ground to the col between Clach Glas and Blaven. Here he turned to the left, and was soon plunging down the screes into the depths of Coire Uaigneich. As he slid down on his heels, first with one foot and then the other, rather as if he were skating, the whole mountain seemed to slide with him, and the noise of the stones was echoed back by the mountain walls until they sounded like a veritable avalanche.

Out of the corrie, flinging itself over the boulders in a series of cascades and waterfalls, a mountain stream had carved a tortuous path. Below the falls the water gathered into deep transparent pools, the floors of which were covered with round pebbles of a beautiful rose colour and green. Jaimie stood for a moment beside one of these, gazing down into the translucent water and watching the trout that nuzzled the pebbles at the bottom. It looked as if he could have put down his hand and caught one, but the clear water was deceptive and was much deeper than it looked.

Suddenly, above the clamour of the cataract, he heard a sound that made him lift his head and scan the lower slopes of the great mountain down whose riven face he had just scrambled—a faint sad cry, that of a lamb in distress. As he watched he saw something moving on a sloping ledge of rock to the right of the gorge. He pulled a small pair of field-glasses out of his rucksack and focused the ledge in them. Yes, it was as he thought—a half-grown lamb, one of the very late-dropped lambs that are often found on the hills. How it had got there he could only guess, since the

14

rock above overhung the ledge, and below was sheer unbroken precipice. Perhaps it had scrambled up somehow along the edge of the gorge, tempted by the carpet of greenest grass that covered the ledge, had managed to gain the ledge and had found it impossible to descend. Anyhow, it was obvious that unless someone went to its rescue it would perish. High in the sky he noticed two black specks, and knew them for a pair of eagles who had their nest on the lower cliffs of Blaven, near the top of a rocky needle, a full six hundred feet above the corrie. Already they had seen the lamb, he guessed, and no doubt they hoped to make a meal of it in due course, even if they did not swoop down and carry it off to their eyrie alive.

Tired as he was, it never occurred to Jamie to leave the lamb to its fate. He turned his back on the distant loch, and began to climb up the edge of the gorge towards the ledge. Sometimes, above the roar of the cataract, he could hear the bleating of the lamb, and the bass 'baa' of its mother, who knew that her offspring was in danger, and was running pathetically to and fro on a flat rocky plateau below. Rowan trees and silver birches overhung the gorge, and great slides of green water came rushing between smooth silvery rock, to fall with shattering crash into deep fernedged pools. All sorts of tiny wild flowers grew in sheltered hollows, together with fat magenta cushions of thyme and tufts of tormentil. In wet places were patches of the lovely Grass of Parnassus, and everywhere was the heady scent of bog-myrtle. It was a beautiful gorge, and at any ordinary time Jaimie would have been the first to stop and admire the loveliness at his feet, for he was a great lover of wild flowers, and indeed of all natural beauty. Now, however, all his thoughts were for the lamb in distress.

He had, by this time, got to the base of the cliff, and an awe-inspiring sight it was, rising in one seemingly unbroken black wall for several hundred feet. Down its face swung a thread of silver, one of the smaller waterfalls that swelled the bigger torrent below. There was also a fissure or narrow ledge, not actually on the main rock face, but which slanted up to the right of it and stopped well above the ledge. It was up this place that Jaimie decided the lamb had climbed, until it had either lost its footing and fallen on to the grassy ledge below, or had half jumped and half slithered there. Wet moss and clumps of ferns and grass grew in cracks as high up as a quarter of the length of the gully, but above this was nothing but barren rock, black and glistening with moisture.

Jaimie studied the place from all angles, then, after depositing his rucksack at the foot of the cliff, he began to 'back up' a short vertical chimney which gave access to the fissure about half-way along its length, and somewhat above the lamb. He climbed up the crack steadily and, when about half way along the grassy ledge, managed to find a spur of rock over which he could pass his rope, so that its two ends hung down over the nearest end of the ledge. After this it was only a matter of minutes before he was standing on the grassy ledge of rock himself. It proved to be very narrow and steeply sloping, whilst above it the cliff overhung in a great beetling crag.

Taking from his pocket a handful of what looked like string but which turned out to be a large bag, very like the old-fashioned string shopping-bags countrywomen take to market, and which he always carried for an emergency such as this, the young man worked himself cautiously along the ledge and caught the lamb. Whereupon he tied its legs together and put it inside the bag. This wasn't as easy as it sounds, because, in spite of its perilous position, the lamb had plenty of fight in it. It regarded its rescuer in the light of an enemy and struggled with all its might to evade capture, and several times nearly fell off the ledge in the process. However it was caught at last, and, as it lay helpless, Jaimie began to consider how he was going to climb down again.

There were obviously two ways—the chimney and the rock face. The chimney appeared impracticable because of the encumbrance of the lamb and the risk of injuring it, so the face it must be, if at all possible. He looked round for another belay. There was a large stone wedged firmly in a crevice, which, when tested, bore his weight. He had already carefully noted a tiny ledge about forty feet below which might be useful if an *abseil* should be possible. The rope, however, would probably jam round the wedged stone which would leave him in a desperate plight on the lower ledge if the rocks below that would not 'go'. There was nothing else for it, however, so he pulled down the rope and hoped for the best, thereby cutting off all hope of a return by way of the fissure. First he cut off a short length

16

*Jaimie worked his way cautiously along the ledge*

to make a loop which he tied round the stone. Then, threading the rope through the loop, he let the two ends hang down the face of the cliff as he had done before.

Slinging the captive lamb over his right shoulder, Jaimie took the double rope in his left hand, standing astride it. Then, with the rope passed round under his right thigh, over his right shoulder and held by his right hand, he *abseiled* down, passing the rope from hand to hand round his body and bracing his feet against the rock face. After this he again pulled down his precious rope, and, thanks be, it did not jam! From the lower ledge he managed to find footholds and safely reached the ground. To an ordinary person the climb might have seemed hair-raising, but to Jaimie Gordon it was all in the day's work.

Having untied its legs he emptied the lamb out of its prison of string, just as a farmer's wife might empty out a stone or two of potatoes, and watched it career across to its anxious parent, who received it with every sign of delight. Then she looked across at Jaimie and 'baa-ed' dismally. It was evident that she regarded him with the utmost disapproval and suspicion. Not for the first time the young man laughed aloud at the queer ways of animals in general, and sheep in particular.

He slung on his rucksack and went on his way. The excitement of the last half an hour had banished his weariness, but by the time he got to the road that wound round the head of the loch it had returned. He reached the shore, and made for a small boat drawn up on the shingle. For a moment he stood quite still, thinking of the mountain top he had just left, and, while he stood there, a car of exceeding brightness and newness proceeded with caution up the stony causeway leading to Airdrochnish Castle on the opposite shore.

'The Slaughters' car,' said Jaimie to himself. 'That will be Deborah Slaughter returning from school with her friend Sheena MacDonald.' Yes, he knew all about the visit, though how he knew, remains one of those mysteries of 'bush telegraphy'.

'Sheena MacDonald,' repeated the young man aloud. 'I am remembering her well.' He had met her once, several years ago, at a *ceilidh* at Ardavasar, near her own village of Glendounie. He had danced with her—she a child of thirteen and he a youth of eighteen, just beginning his studies at the university, but he had not forgotten the grace of her dancing, the wild native dancing of the Isle, nor her strange green eyes. No, he had not forgotten her. . . .

## The Eagles' Nest

THE day after Jaimie's timely rescue of the lamb, Sheena sat at her bedroom window in Castle Airdrochnish. The weather had changed overnight as it so often does in Skye, and now the rain clouds were sweeping over Blaven and mists were hanging on the jagged pinnacles of Clach Glas. High up in Coire Uaigneich she could see the smoke of a waterful, but it was too far away for her to hear the thunder of its swollen waters. It was indeed an awe-inspiring scene, but the girl's thoughts were on other matters. She was thinking about the owner of the castle, Jaimie Gordon, he whom they called Cock o' the North, and wondering if he was indeed as splendid as they said he was. She had met him once, she remembered, but that was a long time ago when she was only a child and before he had become famous as a climber. All the same she hadn't forgotten him, and it was mostly her curiosity that had made her accept Deborah's invitation to stay at the castle, and make one of the Slaughter party for the Skye Gathering Ball tomorrow night. She wanted to meet Jaimie again, and Deborah had said he would be one of the party.

The glossy pages of next month's fashion magazines would be full of the Skye Gathering and the Ball. There would be a special article by Onlooker of *World Fashion* and photographs of many well-known débutantes, with tartan scarves draped over their bare shoulders, accompanied by young men in full Highland evening dress: *The Lady Katriona MacKinnon chooses a quiet spot for a talk with her partner, Dougal MacIntyre of Strathcluanie. . . . Miss Mairi MacLeod and Mr. Robin Scott enjoy a joke together. . . . The lovely Sheena MacDonald, famous throughout the Isle for her beauty, dances the*

*Eightsome Reel with her partner, Jaimie Gordon of Airdrochnish, better known, perhaps, as the Cock o' the North.* . . . Then the writer would go on to relate the daring climbs the young man had done, the rescues he had made. How, when at the University of Edinburgh, he had climbed in the Swiss Alps, in the Austrian Tyrol, in the Himalayas, and how he had made himself familiar with every tough climb in Wales and Scotland.

Yes, thought Sheena complacently, Jaimie Gordon was a fitting person to dance with her at the ball tomorrow night. The first dance it must be—and a few more besides. She went over to the little bureau that stood beside her bed and took out a folded card. It was an invitation card, with a programme of the dances upon it, and opposite, a space for the gentlemen to write their names. The first dance was (oh, how fitting!) the Gay Gordons. Sheena laughed aloud and pencilled in the name 'Jaimie' in the space provided. Deborah was hoping to dance the first dance with him too, she well knew. The guileless and forthright Deborah had said so. 'But he will dance it with *me*,' thought Sheena. 'I shall see that he does.'

And now the question was how to meet the young man? It was fortunate, thought Sheena, that Deborah had chosen to wash and 'set' her hair this afternoon. It might have been difficult to get rid of her. Even as it was, she would have to work quickly. She leaned her white arms on the rugged stone window-sill and wondered where Jaimie lived while his castle was occupied by the Americans. Where did he go all day, and what did he do? Doctored sick animals, she supposed—Deborah had said she thought he was a veterinary surgeon. Where would he be now?

As if in answer to her thoughts, she caught sight of a small boat out on the loch. It was nearing the far side, and in it was a young man. Surely, surely this was he? She ran down to the smoking-room, with its guns, stags' heads and general smell of ancient stone, old leather and dogs, and across to a writing-table that stood in one of the long windows. Ah, here they were! An old pair of field-glasses. She had noticed them when she and Deborah had explored the castle last night. She opened the window softly and focused them on the boat. Yes, it was Jaimie all right. He was just as she remembered him. She watched him draw the boat up on to the seaweedy beach and set off across the

20

moor, where a faint track led towards a plantation of stunted trees—one might almost call them bushes—in which was evidently a house or dwelling of some sort, judging by the plume of smoke that hung in the misty air. She noticed that he was carrying a black bag. Well, said Sheena to herself, he was bound to come back sometime—always provided he didn't actually *live* there.

She ran up to her bedroom again and pulled on an old mackintosh, thanking her lucky stars that Mrs Slaughter took a nap after lunch. As she walked across the room, she caught sight of herself in the old-fashioned gilt mirror over the fireplace, and stopped to admire the picture she made. Yes, she was very beautiful! The pure oval face with its long mysterious green eyes and cloud of tawny hair, the colour of beech trees in autumn, might have belonged to Dante's Beatrix. She had that thick creamy skin that so often goes with red hair, but no single freckle disfigured it. Her figure was slender and graceful, and her head was held proudly on her slim white neck. She sighed with pure delight at her own reflection. Beautiful, beautiful Sheena MacDonald!

Pulling a scarf over her shining hair she tiptoed past the bathroom where, judging from the sounds within, Deborah was still busy with her toilet, and crossing the flagged floor of the square hall let herself out into the storm. Yes, it was storm all right. Yesterday's sunshine had vanished like a dream, and today the tops of the mountains were hidden behind a curtain of slanting rain. The Red Cuillin crouched at the head of the loch like great prehistoric beasts. As for Blaven, his majesty was increased ten-fold by the vapours that boiled and writhed out of his corries and hid his awful head.

Every nerve in Sheena's body thrilled and exulted at the sight of him. Blaven, the mountain she loved best of all the great mountains in Skye! Wild and high-spirited, descendant of a wild and savage clan, she loved this mighty mountain in his every mood, but most of all she loved him in weather like this, when the great gash that seamed his rugged face like an old war-scar stood out dark and glistening, when his many waterfalls thundered down his flanks and the very sky seemed to be weeping over him. The shattered ridge of Clach Glas, jagged as a saw, appeared out of the swirling clouds of mist, then disappeared as if it belonged to a demon world. The savageness of nature, seen in this wild place, struck a similar savage chord in the girl.

She rounded the loch, then left the stony road and took to the moor. She tore off her shoes and stockings and walked barefoot across the cold wet moss and heather, revelling in the feel of it, then took off her scarf and let her hair blow in the rainy wind. She loved the wild place, with its black and glistening precipices, its waterfalls, its shattered ridges piercing the storm clouds.

'A Gordon for me! A Gordon for me!' (she sang)
'If you're no a Gordon, you're no use to me!'

If what she had heard was true, Jaimie Gordon, the Cock o' the North, was indeed the right sort of young man to lead her, Sheena MacDonald, into the ballroom at Portree. Yes, it must be Jaimie and no other.

She found the track he had taken and set off towards the windbreak of trees. On her left, high up above the corrie, rose the lower cliffs of Blaven, predominant amongst them a black and splintered pinnacle, its head lost in the mist. Even as she passed beneath it, a great shadowy bird swept out of the clouds, followed by a second. She could hear the beat of their mighty wings as they cleft the air and soared across the corrie.

'Eagles!' thought Sheena. 'Golden eagles! They must have an eyrie somewhere on that crag.'

Jaimie, returning from doctoring old Murdo MacKinnon's cow which had swallowed a piece of barbed wire and hadn't been able to digest it, saw Sheena when she was quite a long way off. He recognised her instantly. Who else in the Isle had hair that colour? Who else would be walking barefoot in the heather on such a day, and with such freedom and grace? Like many Highlanders, Jaimie possessed the uncanny faculty of being able to see into the future, and, as he walked towards Sheena MacDonald, he had a strange feeling that he was walking towards the girl he would one day marry. Then the feeling was gone, like a dream when the sleeper awakes, and he forgot about it. He knew also that it was no mere chance that had brought her here. He was well aware that she had come in search of him. Meanwhile, he had got to within hailing distance of her. He wondered curiously what would be her pretext for being out here on this wild moor in a storm. Sheena had wondered this herself, and then she had seen the eagles and knew instantly what she was going to say.

She stood in the path, her hair blowing in the wind, and waited for him to come up to her.

'Are you, by chance, Jaimie Gordon?' she said when they met, trying to sound as if she didn't know.

The young man made her a little bow.

'I am,' he said, knowing that she knew.

'I am Sheena,' said the girl. 'Sheena MacDonald. I am staying with the Slaughters at the castle—your castle.'

'I am knowing that already,' said the young man in his soft Highland voice. 'I expect you do not remember me, but we have met before. It was at a *ceilidh* at the little hall at Ardavasar.'

Sheena, as we have said, remembered very well, but her green eyes did not betray the fact.

'Oh, did we? It must have been a very long time ago.'

'It was four years ago,' he said. 'You were only thirteen, but I am remembering you all the same.'

Sheena's lips parted, showing her small and perfect teeth. Things were going well! Jaimie Gordon was evidently of a romantic turn of mind.

'I expect you will be at the Skye Gathering Ball tomorrow night?' she questioned him. 'Deborah and I are going.'

'I shall be there,' said Jaimie. 'By the way, if you are thinking of calling at Uaigneich Cottage to see old Murdo, I am afraid you will not find him at home. He was away to Strathaird when I left.'

'Oh, but I am not going to see anybody,' explained Sheena. 'I came here to see *you*.'

The young man was surprised. He hadn't expected her to be so forthright.

'Yes,' continued Sheena. 'I saw your boat on the loch—at least I guessed it was yours—and I thought you might show me the eagles' nest.' Her eyes lifted to the black pinnacle up in the corrie round which the mists were swirling in tormented clouds.

'How did you know there was an eyrie up there?' asked Jaimie.

'Someone told me about it,' lied Sheena. 'Donald

Gordon, it was. He said he had seen two golden eagles play-ing in the corrie, so I came to find out. Then I saw your boat and I was sure you would know where the eyrie was.'

'Yes, I am knowing,' answered Jaimie. 'It is in a crack in the upper rocks of the pinnacle. You can see it when the mist lifts . . . . There! Do you see the dark hole in the cliff face?'

Sheena studied the black wall with interest. Although she had come out in the first place in search of Jaimie, she was quite ready to add the thrill of finding an eagle's nest to the general excitement.

'Yes, I can see it,' she answered. 'Ah, now it has dis-appeared.' They stood there together in silence, looking upward, but the small cave did not reappear. Finally Sheena's glance fell once more to the young man's dark face.

'If you will climb up there,' she said, looking at him from under her eyelashes, 'if you will climb up to the nest and get for me two eagle's feathers I will wear them in my hair tomorrow night at the ball, and I will give you the first dance besides, Jaimie Gordon.'

Jaimie looked back at her steadily.

'You are knowing that this pinnacle has never been climbed?' he said. 'It is called by climbers "the Unclimbed Pinnacle of Coire Uaigneich". Many have tried, but none has got beyond the Great Slab, three hundred feet up—unless it be one young man whose body we found lying on the screes below, last spring. It is dangerous under good conditions, and I am wearing no proper boots for such a climb. I have no rope, nor companion, and it is misty, and moreover windy. Besides, the rocks will be wet and slippery.'

'But you are Cock o' the North, are you not?' said Sheena, goading him. 'Surely you, Jaimie Gordon, would not let a little small pinnacle like that one beat you?'

'One does not measure the danger of a mountain by its size, nor the inaccessibility of a pinnacle by its height,' Jaimie told her. 'I am not wishful to break my neck for an eagle's feather or two.'

'But you are forgetting the rest of the bargain—the first dance at the ball with me,' put in Sheena. 'But if you are afraid, I shall make an easier bargain with you. If you

24

will climb up there, and if you do not *quite* reach the nest, I will still dance the Gay Gordons with you.'

Jaimie said nothing for a while. He was thinking deeply.

'You shall have your feathers,' he said at last. So saying, he turned on his heel and strode away towards the screes leading to the foot of the pinnacle. Sheena hastily put on her shoes and followed as quickly as she could. Soon the mist swirled about them as they climbed higher into the corrie, hiding the cliffs from their view, but Jaimie led on unerringly until suddenly a great black wall loomed up in front of them.

'This is the foot of the pinnacle face,' said Jaimie. 'If you stay on the left here, close under the rock, you will be safe from any stones I may send down.' He put his bag on the wet ground, while Sheena watched him curiously as he followed the base of the rock wall a little way to the right, where a few nail scratches could be seen ascending an exposed corner of the face. Pausing for a few seconds at this point, he then continued still farther round to the right, and after this began to climb a deep chimney leading up to a broad ledge, finding footholds and handholds where the black precipice seemed unbroken, and finally disappearing into the mist, while the girl stood below, still as a statue, her heart beating fast.

She did not wish him back again. She was thinking of the ball, and the triumph it would be to wear in her hair the feathers of her rank, plucked from the eagles' nest near the top of the Unclimbed Pinnacle of Coire Uaigneich. What a thrill to dance with the man who had conquered that pinnacle! It would all be told in picturesque language by Onlooker of *World Fashion*—she would see that it was! *The beautiful Sheena MacDonald wore her chieftainess's feathers in her auburn hair. Only the day before they had been plucked from the eyrie of the golden eagle on the Unclimbed Pinnacle of Coire Uaigneich by young Jaimie Gordon, the famous Cock o' the North. . . .*

There was no sound in the corrie, except for the faint far-off roar of the waterfall. Then, as she stood listening, she heard a muffled exclamation and a stone fell, dislodged from a cranny or patch of scree high above her head. Jamie must be out on the Great Slab! What if he were to fall and were killed at her feet? What if the eagles were to return? A precariously balanced marauder would stand

25

little chance in an attack by two of the fierce birds defending their sanctuary. But she had seen them fly away (and no doubt Jaimie had seen them too, or he would not have taken the risk), and they would not return for some time. . . . Nevertheless she began to shiver slightly. A cold wind swept down the corrie, and she was wet through. The wild exhilaration that had filled her and kept her warm before, had vanished. She looked at her wrist-watch. It was after five o'clock. She began to wish he would return. . . .

It was nearly an hour later that Jaimie reappeared out of the mist as silently as a shadow. From out of his coat pocket he took two eagle's feathers and handed them to her without a word. Then he walked back to the place where he had left his bag and picked it up.

'I have got the feathers for you,' he said at length, 'because I would not have it said that Sheena MacDonald was calling the Cock o' the North a coward, but as for the ball —when I am wishful to dance with a lassie I shall not be waiting for her to ask *me*.' So saying, he again made her the stiff little bow with that native dignity possessed by every Highlander, be he laird or gillie. 'And if I were not in so great a hurry,' he added, turning back to her, 'I should be giving one small wayward lassie a piece of my mind as well.'

He turned on his heel and strode off down the corrie, leaving her to follow him or not, just as she thought fit.

## The Skye Gathering Ball

THE resident guests at the Sligachan Hotel had finished dinner and were enjoying their coffee in the lounges, but it was obvious that other diners were expected later on. The tables had been laid again with fresh snowy cloths, vases of flowers and ferns, and sparkling wine-glasses. Moreover at the places where the ladies were to sit lay small nosegays of exquisite tiny wild mountain flowers, each with a sprig of bog-myrtle for fragrance, and a sprig of rowan to keep away the evil sprites of Skye, The guests were evidently important ones!

At an unobtrusive table in a far corner sat a small man with keen grey eyes that saw everything, though they appeared to be scanning the menu-card at his elbow. This was Onlooker from *World Fashion*, sent from London especially to give his impressions of the Skye Gathering Ball.

Many of the guests, living in far corners of the island, had arranged to meet at this hotel and have dinner there before going on to Portree where the dance was held; and, besides these, there were quite a number who had arrived the day before and were staying here over the week-end. The journalist looked round the charming dining-room and noted the many beautiful pictures upon the walls. They were all original water-colours, done by famous artists who had come here to paint, and who had fallen in love with Skye and her mountains. There were pictures of the Cuillin Hills in every mood. Here Sgurr nan Gillian (the Peak of the Young Men) gazed at her own graceful reflection in a mountain tarn at the foot of Glen Sligachan. Over there, round-browed Masco shone, rosy hued, in the early morning light. Here was Blaven from Glen Sligachan; Blaven from Loch Slapin, and dark Loch Coruisk, hidden in a recess of the Black Cuillin. Here was Sgurr Alasdair, monarch of the mountains, with a crown of snow upon his brow, and at his feet, remote Lochan Coire Lagan. Every mood and every season had been caught by the artist's brush—the Cuillin in spring and in summer, veiled in autumn mists, white with winter snow. Always the Cuillin—the magic hills of Skye!

Onlooker had just finished examining them all when the doors were flung open, and in came the expected guests—a crowd of laughing girls and men, all dressed in the gayest of clothes, the men outdoing the girls in the splendour of full Highland evening-dress. The party that interested the reporter most was the table next to his own. Some of these people were obviously Americans—he could tell that easily enough, even if he hadn't been near enough to hear them speak. Their frank and open enjoyment gave them away. Their manners were so very different, thought Onlooker, from the reticence and reserve of the High-

27

lander. Of course you must remember, added Onlooker to himself, that America is a youthful nation, whereas the Highlands of Scotland (and this island in particular) are as old as Time itself. This phrase pleased him and he jotted it down on the back of the menu-card, adding a few words about 'wrapped in the mists of Ossian, the Gaelic poet'.

With a growing sense of disappointment the reporter listened to the chatter of the resplendent guests. All these young men in their kilts and velvet jackets, their laces and their dirks, talked to each other in the most impeccable English public-school voices! Not one of them betrayed his Scottish birth by a single syllable. Moreover, even what they *said* was English in the extreme. . . . 'Tell you what, old man'—this from one young man to a fellow kinsman, both of them in full Highland dress—'the traffic problem in London is gettin' to be more than a joke. Got stuck in a street off Oxford Circus last week, and a Yankee in a dashed great automobile the size of the Albert Memorial backed right into me. Yes, would you believe it? Did I stand on the horn! I'm telling you! Chap didn't as much as look round. . . .' 'Oh, how-do, McLane! Fancy meetin' you here! Thought you were too dashed busy to tear yourself away from the daily grind. . . .' 'What's that? Did I get my *what*? My *degree*? Good lord, no! Not on your life! Not even a "Third". Turfed out, old chap, neck and crop. Thrown out on the ear! Didn't appreciate me at Oxford, it seems! What am I goin' to do now? Silly sort of question to ask, if you'll excuse my saying so. Work, I suppose. . . .'

Onlooker sighed. The girls were worse if anything, their voices even more determinedly English. He decided that he preferred the nasal tones of the Americans at the next tables. At least they were themselves, and were not ashamed to be so.

'Say, Momma,' drawled one of the girls of the party, 'take a look at these cute little bunches of flowers! Do we have to wear them? W-aal—what d'yer know! There's a little brooch to fasten them in with, and guess what—it's in the tartan! Talk about fascinating! They must have seen you coming, Momma! Say—d'you suppose it's the custom in Skye always to give folks little nosegays at dinner parties?'

'I wouldn't know, I guess, dear,' answered Mrs

28

Slaughter, smiling across at her pretty excited young daughter. 'You'd better ask Mr Gordon here. He sure ought to know, being an Islander himself.'

'Oh, Momma,' pouted Deborah, 'do you have to keep on calling him "mister". It's much too formal, especially when' (she blushed deliciously) 'he's my partner for this evening. He's "Jamie" to us, aren't you, Jamie? We *are* allowed to call you by your first name, aren't we?'

'I am being most honoured,' said Jaimie Gordon in his soft voice. He was far too polite to explain that, being the laird of Airdrochnish, the 'mister' was incorrect in any case.

Onlooker glanced up quickly. Here at last was a young man who didn't speak with an English public-school accent! How refreshing! Then the names struck a chord in his trained memory . . . Gordon . . . Jaimie. . . . Why, this must be the celebrated climber, Jaimie Gordon, known as Cock o' the North. His interest in the next table grew at every moment. By the conversation he gathered that the dark handsome young Scot was the partner of the fresh-faced American girl. A pity, he thought. The other girl would have suited him so much better—the lovely girl in the sparkling white dress, like frost on snow (he described it mentally), that set off her vivid Titian beauty to perfection. What a pair they would have made! A great pity! He resolved to get a photograph of the party, and some-how he would contrive to get Jamie Gordon next to the girl in white, partner or no partner. Onlooker had a keen sense of beauty and of the dramatic. Moreover he was as unscrupulous as journalists usually are! . . . *The famous Cock o' the North, Jaimie Gordon, and his partner, the lovely Titian-haired Miss —— (he must find out who she was) resting after an especially lively strathspey.*

It certainly looked at the moment as if Sheena was going to get her picture in *World Fashion* all right, and with the young man of her choice also!

Portree is only nine miles north of Sligachan, so it didn't take the Slaughters' high-powered automobile long to cover that distance. Some way behind, swaying and bump-ing over the moorland road, came Onlooker in his old and battered Ford, determined to see all there was to see. So it happened that when the female members of the Slaughter

29

party came out of the cloakroom into the lobby of the Skye Gathering Hall, to join their male escorts, the indefatigable journalist was just in time to see a small black-haired girl, dressed in an old mackintosh, which had part of the hem undone, dart over to a door leading to the, cloakrooms. Half way across the lobby she nearly had a head-on collision with the Airdrochnish party.

'Annette Dancy!' exclaimed Sheena. 'Whatever are *you* doing here?'

The small girl stopped short and stared.

'Sheena! Whatever are *you* doing here?' she said in her turn.

The Scots girl recovered first from her surprise. She didn't introduce Annette to the men of the party, but turned to Mamie Slaughter and Deborah.

'This is Annette Dancy,' she explained to her hostess. 'She's a ballet-dancer, and my uncle is vicar of Annette's parish in Northumberland.'

'But whatever are you doing here?' said Annette again. 'I thought you were at school in Edinburgh.'

'Deborah and I have come over for the ball,' said Sheena. 'This is the Skye Gathering, you know, and after all Skye is my home, so it isn't really so astonishing that I should be here. But you, Annette—I thought you were in London.'

'So I was. So I am,' said Annette. 'But you see, we're touring Scotland, and when they wanted a ballet for the cabaret tonight they asked us. I mean my company, of course. It's the junior part of the company,' she added honestly. 'In fact it's just the school, really.'

'I didn't know there was going to be a cabaret, or that it was going to be a ballet. What is the ballet called, anyway?' asked Sheena.

'It's *La Sylphide*,' answered Annette, hopping this way and that so as to get out of the way of passing guests, and incidentally looking very much out of place in her ancient mackintosh. Onlooker, being, as we have said, intensely aware of the dramatic side of a situation, scented drama here. His eyes dwelt upon Annette's muddy flat-heeled shoes, and next to them Sheena's silver sandals, composed of a minimum of slender straps. Yet in Annette's clod-hopping shoes were the feet of a dancer. He knew it, even before she said with a proud toss of her head, 'And

*I'm* in the ballet. As a matter of fact, although I know you won't believe it, I'm La Sylphide. I can hardly believe it myself, but it's true.'

Onlooker knew that it was true. The way she moved, the gestures she made. Who could doubt that she was indeed a dancer?

The male members of the Slaughter party began to grow interested. There was something about this funny child that was strangely fascinating.

'I always thought it was *Les Sylphides*—with an "s",' said a fair young man, the fourth member of the party, not including Mamie and her husband. He was officially Sheena's partner, since Jaimie had appropriated Deborah. 'Also I thought there was no main rôle in that ballet but a number of *solos, pas de deux*, and so on.'

Annette turned to him, with respect for his knowledge and tolerance for his ignorance.

'Most people think they're one and the same ballet,' she explained. 'But I assure you they are not. *Les Sylphides* is all that is left to us of the original ballet *La Sylphide*. The ignorance of the public is really abysmal,' she added loftily. 'I mean, of course, balletically. Well, if you will please excuse me, I really must go now. It's quite time I was made-up.'

She disappeared through the door, leaving the young man looking after her in astonishment.

'What a very peculiar child,' he remarked. 'But I suppose she's right.' He drew the attention of the rest of the party to a poster which had been pinned up over the fireplace of the lobby. 'It certainly says *La Sylphide* here.'

'Yes, and it says the rôle of La Sylphide will be danced by Simonetta Delgarno,' put in Sheena quickly. 'So it can't be true what Annette said—that she was dancing the chief rôle. I thought it couldn't be. Why, she's only just started.'

But it *was* true, nevertheless, and if you want to know how it came about, you must leave the Highland ball for a short time and come with me to London.

FROM Portree, the capital of Skye, to Leicester Square in London is a very long way. By ordinary means of travel it would take you at least two days to get from the one to the other. But an author doesn't need to rely on ferry-boats and trains, and can therefore do the same journey in as many minutes. An author isn't bound by time either, so let's go back a couple of months to a certain hot day at the beginning of July, and stroll into Leicester Square in the heart of London.

Sitting on a seat under the welcome shade of the plane trees, surrounded by a crowd of hopeful sparrows, sat a small dark-haired girl eating a ham sandwich. It was a large thick sandwich, with a great deal of bread and not much ham inside, and perhaps that was why Annette had given most of it to the sparrows. Two of these sandwiches and an apple composed her lunch, and she had the same every day, except that the 'filling' in the sandwiches might be different. The Sisters in the Convent Home where Annette stayed, and who put up the lunches, were well meaning but lacked imagination. Annette's mother, who was a clergyman's widow, had thought that a Convent Home would be the safest place in wicked old London to house her fifteen-year-old daughter while she continued her studies as a ballet-dancer, and no doubt she was right. Although Annette might be lonely when she went home at night to that silent austere building, with its endless flights of uncarpeted stairs, its bare parquet floors and its devout nuns, all busily praying for the wicked world, at least she had peace and quiet. Her tiny cell-like bedroom was furnished with a narrow iron bedstead, one chair and a corner wardrobe, composed of a rail with a curtain hung across. A small chest-of-drawers did duty for a dressing-table, and upon it were arranged many snapshots, framed in passe-partout, of Annette's family and all her many friends. She had had a job to find room for her brush and comb! The glass of the photographs was smeared, owing to Annette's habit of kissing her family when she went to bed at night!

32

Annette's bedroom was on the fifth floor, and out of the tiny window one had a view of miles and miles of chimney-pots of every shape and size, a view broken here and there by the top of a tall church steeple. Many of these had clocks in them, and at the hour, half-hour and sometimes at the quarter-hour too, Annette listened to quite an orchestra of chimes in every key, and in all sorts of tones, from the deep faraway boom of Big Ben to the silvery chime of a famous city clock opposite the Home. On the floor below was the Mother Superior's bedroom, which had a french window opening out on to a little roof-garden. By screwing round in her window-seat Annette could just manage to see a clump of flowering heath, and, by stretching her imagination to the utmost, she could make herself believe she was at home in her own little bedroom that looked out over the wild Northumbrian moorland.

In the evening, when the sun stole round and fell upon one corner of her window-seat, Annette used to curl up there, close her eyes and think of her home, Dancing Peel, her darling mother, Maximilian her brother, and all the people she knew and loved in the little village of Mintlaw. Oh, how she missed them! How she longed for them! The tears would steal down her nose when she thought of Old Sally Muirhead who lived in Postie's Cottage with Timmy, her three-legged cat; of Bella, with her deep rumbling Northumbrian voice, who helped to do the work in the old peel-house. Sometimes when she went to bed she dreamt she was roaming the Border hills with Maximilian, or Angus, the vicar's son, or picking blackberries maybe, or practising her dancing on the flat roof of the old Border fortress. At the back of her dream lurked a Titian-haired girl with long mysterious green eyes—Sheena MacDonald, Angus's cousin. Annette didn't like or understand Sheena, and this was perhaps why, in Annette's dreams, Sheena always lurked in the background and never came out into the open.

Annette wasn't dreaming of her home now, however, as she sat under the trees in Leicester Square. She was thinking of Monsieur Georges, her ballet-master, and his mime class. She had learnt a little classical mime at her Newcastle dancing-school, and had always been told not to make it *too* dramatic. But Monsieur Georges had different

33

ideas. He was the very essence of drama himself, and he liked drama, even in his mime classes.

'I *keel* myself!' he would say aloud, miming at the same time. 'I say *keel*, not *loff*! Make 'im *look* like keel! Oh, you Eengleesh girls, you 'ave no idea of ze drama. Of you all, Annette Dancy ees not 'alf bad. . . . Now say, "Ow I *loff* you!" No, no, *no*! I say *"loff"*! What you do there might mean anysings, or nozzings. Annette Dancy ees a quarter good, but not so good as "keel". Do 'im once more a time. . . .'

Annette loved Monsieur Georges from the bottom of her ballet-loving heart. Here was no schoolgirl 'crush', no film-star adoration. She loved him with her whole being, just as she loved her home, or her mother, or a beautiful picture. She didn't expect anything in return. He was a god on a pedestal, as far above ordinary people as Nelson on his column. When he lifted his ascetic face, with its highly bridged nose and sensitive nostrils, and so much as glanced in her direction, Annette's whole being thrilled, just as if she were a harp and he a musician plucking the strings.

'He's so *beautiful*,' thought Annette, as he demonstrated a movement. 'All his thoughts are beautiful ones too. You can tell that when he dances. He's thinking all the time of the beauty of the movement, of the music, the art. He never thinks of ugly things like—like trolley-buses, or dustbins, or gasometers, or blocks of flats.' It will be seen that some of the aspects of city life had impressed Annette with their ugliness.

As she thought about Monsieur Georges and his mime class, Annette was unconsciously going through the movements. . . . 'I—me—*kill*!' she said with passion, clenching her fist on an imaginary dagger-hilt and thrusting the blade into her quivering bosom.

A man sitting on the opposite end of the seat watched her, fascinated, wondering if she had, by chance, got St Vitus's Dance or some other nervous ailment.

'Are you all right, little girl?' he said anxiously a length.

Annette jumped—and came all the way back from Monsieur Georges's studio to Leicester Square with a bump.

'A-all right?' she repeated. 'Oh—yes, I—I think so. What do you mean?'

'You were doing some very funny things,' said the

34

interested gentleman. 'Like this.' He imitated as well as he could Annette's antics.

Annette burst out laughing.

'Oh, *that*! I was just killing myself,' she explained airily, and wondered why the friendly gentleman drew back as if he had been stung. 'It's not as easy as you'd think,' she added. 'Not the way Monsieur Georges wants it done.'

Fortunately just at this moment a diversion was caused by a young man who burst into their midst with a volley of English and French exclamations, and a few Spanish ones to make weight. Sparrows flew in all directions and settled on the plane trees above, chattering their disapproval.

'Annette, *chérie*! How good it is to see you again!'

'Maximilian!' exclaimed Annette, throwing her arms round her brother's neck, and bursting into tears as she always did in moments of extreme happiness. 'Oh, Max, you don't know how I've missed you! You don't know how homesick and lonely I get sometimes! It isn't that I don't like London. I adore it, but I miss you all so much. Oh, Maxie—now you're here I shall be quite, quite happy. How is the Spanish dancing going, and did you like Spain?'

'Oh, how I was in my true element!' said the young man. 'It was altogether *admirable. Vraiment c'était une belle affaire!* And guess what, Annette—I've got a "spot"!'

The interested gentleman on the other end of the seat scanned the speaker's flawless olive complexion, and decided that he was as mad as the little girl. He had no spot —not even a pimple. How was a mere Londoner to know that a 'spot' in theatrical language means a place in the limelight. Annette knew that her brother meant he had been given, if not a *solo*, then a *pas de deux*, or some other dance of importance.

'Oh, Max, I am thrilled! You *are* lucky!' she said. Then she gave a little sigh.

'Well, so are you,' answered Maximilian. 'You *did* get that part you were telling me about—one of the spirits or something in your new ballet, *La Sylphide*?'

Annette sighed again.

'Oh, yes, I got it all right, but you would hardly call it a "spot". Madame Boccaccio came into class—she's doing the rehearsing until Monsieur Georges is ready for us, you know—and chose out the sylphs. There are twelve of them in the ballet, you know, besides La Sylphide herself. Well, she chose out eleven, and then she said, "Now we are one short, eh? *Que faire?* What to do? There ees no-one—*no*-one who could de eet. . . . Ah, ze leetle small child over there" (that was me, Maxie, *me*, and I'm fifteen,' wailed Annette, 'and then she only noticed me because someone pointed me out!) "she ees ze on-ly one left, and she 'as 'ad no experience. Ah, well, eet must be 'er, since there ees no-one else". It wasn't exactly a triumph, Max—to be chosen just because there's nobody else. I call it a positive insult myself. Me, Annette Dancy, the most beautiful dancer in all Northumberland!'

Annette's arrogance passed over Maximilian's head. He had too much of it himself to notice.

'No, I suppose you couldn't call it a triumph,' he admitted. 'Still, you've only been at the ballet-school for about five minutes, so you couldn't expect them to give you a "spot" quite yet. By the way, who's got the main rôle, La Sylphide?'

'A girl called Simonetta Delgarno,' said Annette. 'She's Italian, but her mother's French, and I think myself she's rather good but most frightfully conceited. *She* thinks she's the most beautiful dancer that has ever lived, bar none.' (Annette said this quite seriously. It never occurred to her that perhaps Annette Dancy might be called the tiniest bit conceited too.) 'She's been in the Marquis de Cuevas Ballet, so of course she thinks she knows *everything*! Matter of fact, she doesn't look a bit like a sylph, and she doesn't dance like one either. She's far too *French*, if you see what I mean. French people just *don't* look like sylphs—they're far too *chic*. Whoever saw a *chic* sylph?'

Maximilian had to laugh—Annette's little face was so serious.

'Don't forget you're half French yourself,' he teased her, 'though nobody could accuse *you* of being *chic*—not in that old print frock!'

'Oh, I know I'm partly French, but I'm part Northumbrian too,' said Annette, ignoring the insult to her appearance, 'and that's the bit that would be just perfect for La Sylphide.'

'Are you suggesting, by any chance, that you should dance the chief rôle?' inquired Maximilian.

'Well, I could do the Scottish steps in the *solos* beautifully,' answered Annette. 'You can't deny it, Max.'

'If you take my advice, you'd better start learning to do the *corps de ballet* bits beautifully too, *chère amie*, or you'll be getting chucked out of *that*,' advised Maximilian.

These words were not quite so wise, or so prophetic as Max thought, as will be seen by after events.

'Oh, by the way,' Annette said, after they had both been silent for some little time, 'I do hope you've had lunch, Maxie. I've eaten all mine. At least I've given most of it to the sparrows.'

'I had it before I came to find you,' said Maximilian.

'And come to that, how *did* you find me?' she asked curiously.

'Easy!' laughed her brother. 'Only needed a little detective work. I knew for a start that you often came here to eat your grub, so I dropped off a bus at the corner and asked a policeman if he'd seen a girl with a far away look in her eye walking along doing an *entrechat* occasionally, and he directed me straight here. Said he'd "shadowed" you for quite a bit, wondering if you were feeble-minded or just an eccentric, or maybe out to commit a crime!'

Annette burst out laughing. Maximilian's description was too true!

'Tell you what, though,' he went on, 'I'll stand you an ice-cream at that place off Piccadilly Circus, if you like—provided you don't choose one over two bob.'

'Oh, Max—how sweet of you!' cried Annette. 'I was just feeling like a sundae. It must be the sandwiches—they *were* a bit dry! There's just time before my rehearsal —it's at half past two. You can come back with me, if you like.'

'O.K. Come on then,' said Max. '*Dépêche-toi, mon enfant!*'

'How long are you here for?' asked Annette, as they dashed round the Square and out into Coventry Street. 'In England, I mean?'

'Oh, quite a bit,' said Maximilian. 'We finish where we are tomorrow night. Then we go to Bournemouth and several other south-coast towns. After that, strangely

enough, we're taking over *your* theatre for a month. . .
Come on, we'd better cross here.'

'That's the month the company's going abroad, and we
—the school, I mean—will be on our Scottish tour.' Annette
said when they were safely on the other side of the road.
'We're visiting Sunderland and Newcastle on our way.
Imagine it! I shall be dancing in a real theatre in my own
home town, and I shall see Mummy and dear old Dancing
Peel. I haven't seen the Peel since Christmas, because at
Easter I hadn't any holiday so Mummy came to London
instead. Poor Mummy! I think she'll be awfully glad when
all the dividing alterations that are being done to the Peel
are finished, and she can go back there to live. She must
hate having to live in the middle of a town while they are
being done, though of course it's been sweet of Aunt
Molly to have her there, and thank goodness it was the
winter mostly.'

Annette chattered away, completely unaware of the fact
that she was attracting the attention of the passers-by
with her vivid and expressive face. Or perhaps it was Maximilian—handsome vivacious Max, with his dark flashing
eyes and haughty nose. Or maybe just the two of them together.

'It will be useful having her at Aunt Molly's while the
company is in Newcastle,' observed Maximilian as they
paused on the island in the middle of Piccadilly Circus.
'You'll be able to stay there at nights instead of having to
scratch round for digs.'

'Yes, it will be lovely,' agreed his sister. 'And at the
week-end, we're going to Mintlaw to stay in Angus's cottage. I mean, the one that his father lives in.' She sighed
happily. 'As Saturday happens to be my free day, I shall
have two whole days there. It makes me want to cry just to
think of it!'

'Shouldn't do that, old girl,' said Max. 'Not here anyway. Too much water as it is!' He glanced up at Eros's
statue with its fountains. 'You might cause an overflow!
Come on, now. Traffic has eased up a bit.' They dodged
across the Circus and into the welcome shade of the big
shops of Regent Street with their awnings.

'By the way, talking of this tour of yours,' went on
Maximilian. 'I can't quite see how you can go on a tour
when you're only a ballet-school?'

'Oh, it's only a small tour,' admitted Annette. 'Monsieur Georges thinks it does us good to have a little experience, and we *do* have classes every morning as well as rehearsals. We work jolly hard, I can tell you.'

'How do you know?' teased Max. 'You haven't started it yet.'

'I've been told,' Annette said loftily.

'Well, here's the ice-cream place,' put in Maximilian. 'We've just got twenty minutes. What towns are you visiting in Scotland?'

'As a matter of fact,' said Annette, perching herself on a high stool and studying the brightly coloured menu-card in front of her, 'although it's called a Scottish tour, we're doing a couple of Lancashire towns to start off with, besides Sunderland and Newcastle. After that I think it's to be Selkirk and Galashiels, and then Glasgow. We're going to Edinburgh too for a week, because it's their Festival, but of course we're not at one of the really *big* theatres,' she added modestly. 'If we're a success we may go farther north. Someone said we might visit Fort William. That would be marvellous, wouldn't it? I've never been to the Highlands.'

'Sounds all right,' agreed Maximilian. 'Have you decided what you're going to have? I hate to hurry you, old girl, but we've only ten minutes left if we're to be in time for your rehearsal.'

'Gosh, so we have!' sighed Annette. 'It's awfully hard to choose, isn't it—they all look so nice. Peach melba looks wonderful, but it's half a crown, and anyway I expect they'll only be tinned peaches. I think I'll play safe and have a banana split,' she added to the waitress who had appeared at her elbow. 'What about you, Max?'

'Orange fandango for me,' Maximilian said, Spanish to the last!

IN a tall narrow street leading off Oxford Circus stands
a shabby old-fashioned building with Victorian pillars
and portico, and a wrought-iron sign above saying,
GALAXY THEATRE. It was here that the Cosmopolitan Ballet
had its home. It didn't give performances there every
night, or even every week, but, between tours in the provinces and abroad, it performed in this theatre more or
less regularly. Financially (even with help from the Arts
Council) it was finding it hard to keep its head above
water, so, while it toured the provinces and took an
occasional trip across the Atlantic to earn dollars, the
theatre was let to other companies. The auditorium would
resound no longer to the faint tap-tap of point shoes, but
with Gipsy Flamenco dance music, the click of the cast-
anets, as Spanish dancers filled the stage with noise and
colour. After this would come the soft clash of silver ank-
lets, ear-rings and bracelets, as Indian dancers took over
the theatre, to the sound of their sad, wailing music. Sometimes the vibrating drum-beats of African folk-dancing filled
the place; at other times the stage was crowded with rubber
mackintoshes and hobble-skirts, as exponents of Modern
Ballet performed Frankie and Johnnie tragedies.

But it is not with the actual theatre that we are concerned just now, but with the ballet-school—that famous
school ruled over by Monsieur Georges, Annette's hero.
'Ruled' is the right word. Monsieur Georges was a despot if
ever there was one. Absolute monarch of his little domain
was the ballet-master. He might almost be said to hold the
powers of life and death in his hands, since the authority
to dismiss a student from the school was his, and what was
this but death? His name was inscribed in faint letters
on a brass plate by the side of the stage-door which said
simply:

MONSIEUR GEORGES REINHOLT DUTOIT—ECOLE DE DANSE

No letters after his name. No embellishments. Monsieur

Georges did not need them. He was known through the dancing world. Note the absence of reference to 'Tap' or 'Musical Comedy'. Monsieur Georges scorned these things. He was Russian trained and would have no 'boogie-woogie' in *his* studio!

Although Russian born he had left that country long ago, and conducted his classes mostly in the French language, or in broken English. Only when at a loss to express himself in either of these languages did he resort to his native tongue. The ballet-master's surname, Dutoit, was certainly appropriate. So said his students, as they climbed up to their classes. Up the echoing stone stairs they panted, past the star dressing-rooms, drab and dusty but alive with ghosts for any who had the imagination to see them; past the dressing-rooms of the soloists and the coryphées, and up to the long dormitory-like rooms of the Ladies of the Corps de Ballet. 'Up! Up! Excelsior!' as one young student laughed, breathing hard. 'Only a few more storeys and we're there!' Past the big barn of a room where old Arabelle spent her tireless days ironing tarlatans, mending tears, tending the hundreds of costumes that were in her care, for she combined the duties of wardrobe-mistress with that of caretaker. 'Up! Up! We're nearly there—only a few more steps, and here it is!' Yes, this is the famous ballet-studio of Monsieur Georges Reinholt Dutoit, known and loved by dancers throughout the world. Nearly as famous, this studio, as Sadler's Wells and almost as difficult to enter, for Monsieur Georges could pick and choose his students, and did so ruthlessly. Moreover Monsieur Georges couldn't and wouldn't stand visitors. Not that many had the tenacity (or the breath) to climb up those seven flights of stone stairs to his ballet-school on the roof of London, but if, by chance, they did arrive there, down they went again, quick march, a great deal quicker than they had come up! Monsieur Georges would have none of them—not even the BBC or the movie men had so far managed to invade his domain.

The studio had three dormer windows, between which were long mirrors, with yet more mirrors facing them on the bare wall opposite. There was a grand piano on a low *estrade*, *barres* on the three sides, and a movable *barre* that fitted into sockets in the middle of the floor and was used by students for *pas de deux* work. That was all. There were no chairs. Monsieur Georges did not allow his students to sit down between exercises and *enchaînements*. If they were exhausted they lay down on the floor. It was much better for the muscles.

A door led out of the studio on to the roof. Here on warm days, dressed in bathing-costumes, the students sunbathed or practised their dancing. You would be amazed at the life that went on up here among the chimney-pots. Opposite the ballet-school windows were the windows of the top floor of a world-famous dress house. In those attic rooms many a creation that would adorn film star or society beauty were worked out by designers, and handsewn by the industrious and nimble fingers of an army of work-girls.

On the far side was a sculptor's studio. Day after day Monsieur Georges's students could see the sculptor chipping away at his bust, or statue, or whatever it was. Sometimes it was a whole group of figures, and what intrigued Annette and her companions was how he managed to get his massive work down all those stairs! Between two round chimney-cowls on the other side was a photographer's workroom, and to the left, behind the large red stack, a typewriting agency plied its trade. On warm days, when all the windows were open, the tap-tap of the industrious typists vied with the tap-tap of the ballet-students in their blocked shoes! Yes, there was a whole little world up here among the roof-tops!

It was really very peaceful up here, away from the roar of London's traffic, and the only disadvantage was, as Annette said, the smuts that lay upon everything. After an hour or so on the roof you needed a bath straightaway. Yet in spite of the smuts and the smoke, the sun managed to get through to the roof of this tall building with a heat and brightness that was quite unbelievable. Old Arabelle had a great bush of yellow broom in a tub outside her door (she lived up here too in an attic with a large dormer window and a blue door leading out on to the roof) and a white jasmine climbed up the wall behind it, filling the air with scent on wet evenings. She also had a forest of geraniums in window-boxes, and they were a sight to behold. But then, as Paddy Dolan, Annette's Irish friend, said, 'Arabelle has green fingers, the darlint!'

They all loved old Arabelle. She was no ordinary domestic, though she kept the studio so clean and brightly polished that you could lie on the floor without getting so much as a mark on your *tutu* or cross-over cardigan, no matter how light the colour—no mean feat up here on the smutty roof-top!

Yes, they all (the girl students, I mean), wore *tutus*—even for classes. When Monsieur Georges had taught in Rome, in Paris, and in (unpronounceable name!), all the girls had worn *tutus*. He saw no reason why they should not do so now. He detested those *trunks*. The very name was *tout à fait révoltant!* He liked his pupils to *look* like dancers. Then perhaps they might ('I repeat the "might",' adds Monsieur Georges) with a lot of practice, a lot of fortitude and a great big lot of luck, *become* dancers. One never knew. Miracles had been known to happen.

Dramatic, sarcastic, dynamic Monsieur Georges! How they loved him! How they worked for him! How they hung upon his every scathing word, and every lordly gesture—even to the way he caught up the water-can that stood in a corner of the studio, and swung it to water the floor and make it less slippery, or flung down a handful of rosin into the rosin-box in the other corner, and crushed it underfoot, or ran one long sensitive hand through his bristly black hair! All of them, that is, except Simonetta. She, as Annette had told Maximilian, was half French, half Italian, and she had been in the De Cuevas company, and so considered herself a dancer in her own right. She seemed to be more amused than awed by Monsieur Georges. To put it into her own broken English, 'How he is *drôle*, that one there!' she would exclaim, with a shrug of her expressive shoulders. 'He want me to *arabesque* in all ze wrong place! When I dance at La Scala in Rome, I do eet not so, but *so*.' Yes, she had the temerity to argue with him; to put him right—he, Georges Reinholt Dutoit, old enough to be her father! *'Quelle idée!'* The company were fascinated. It was like watching a small mischievous child poking a tiger between the bars of his cage, when the bars of the cage were made not of steel but of cardboard. They expected every minute to see Monsieur Georges tear down the cardboard and annihilate Simonetta, but up to the present the worst hadn't happened. So far they were still circling each other warily, rather like two practised boxers in the ring, each neasuring the other's strength.

43

And now the rehearsals for the new ballet, *La Sylphide*, had begun in earnest. Simonetta was to dance the chief rôle, naturally. For one thing she knew the ballet, and had danced in it with De Cuevas. True, she had only been in the *corps de ballet*, but had she not watched Hightower, and Golovine? Moreover, in the De Cuevas company one was still an individual even though one was only in the *corps*. . . .

'*C'est vrai, ça!*' exclaimed the exasperated Monsieur Georges. 'How I know eet! No discipline, no restraint! Everyone doing just what they weesh, and no-one thinking about ze ballet as a whole. Besides, I do not 'old wiz the De Cuevas version of zat ballet. There ees none of Scottish feeling in it. Behold ze keelts—skirts, or what you call them—all of them of ze *couleur pastel*! It goes not so in Scotland. I 'ave been there. I *know*. I 'old not wiz ze choreography of Anna Ricardo *non plus*. Zere are liberties which she 'as take wiz zat ballet zat nevaire in ze Danish ballet would be allow'. In ze first act, *par exemple*, La Sylphide in *arabesque penchée*. Nevaire, nevaire! She must be on her knee as in ze *peinture*. In ze Ballet des Champs Elysées eet ees more true, yes. Roland Petit 'as follow more complete ze Bournonville choreography. But De Cuevas—*non, non pas!* Other ballets, yes, but *La Sylphide*, no. She goes not!'

The rehearsal would proceed. Simonetta would bow to the inevitable (the will of the ballet-master and choreographer), and all would be well. But Monsieur Georges took only one rehearsal a week at the moment. The rest were taken by Madame Boccaccio. She was putting in the spade-work, if one can say that of a ballet. At these rehearsals Simonetta was left to go her own sweet way. Madame Boccaccio did not appreciate the finer points of the Bournonville choreography, which Monsieur Georges was following so closely, or if she did, it suited her to forget the details. She was (let's whisper it) more than a little afraid of the temperamental Simonetta. Let Monsieur Georges deal with that one, thought Madame, glancing at the girl's beautiful sulky face.

Monsieur Georges's rule of barring all onlookers from his roof-top studio didn't apply to dancers, of course. Students from all over the world gathered there, and joined in his classes for the moderate sum of five shillings a class if they could afford it, or nothing at all if they couldn't. So when Annette and Maximilian arrived at the stage-door of the Cosmopolitan Theatre, they hurried in without pausing.

'He'll adore you, Maxie,' prophesied Annette, 'He loves anything spectacular (and you must admit you're *that*, Max), and he loves Spanish dancing—especially Flamenco. Come quickly, Maxie! I'm late already. Oh, dear, why did I eat any of those sandwiches! These stairs don't lend themselves to sandwiches—not the sort Sister Angelica cuts anyway.'

On the landing in the middle of the seventh flight they met Monsieur Georges himself.

'This is my brother, Maximilian Léopold Duchène Dancy,' said Annette grandly, determined to make an impression. 'He wants to watch the rehearsal, if you don't mind. He's——'

Monsieur Georges brushed her explanation aside. There was no need of it. Of course, of course the young man was a dancer. There was no doubt about that. The very way he walked, the way he stood there—beautiful as a bronze statue—betrayed him for what he was.

'*Bien! Bien!*' he said with a nod of approval for the young man's strength, his supple grace, his handsome mobile features. Monsieur Georges was, as we have said, an ardent beauty-lover, and here before him was something rare indeed—the completely perfect male human form. No wonder he murmured '*Bien!*'

The roof studio was filled with noise—the clamour of people all talking together in a dozen different languages.

'This is Charles—he's dancing James,' Annette explained, as a young man in black tights and open-neck shirt strolled out of the dressing-room. 'Charles, this is my brother, Maximilian. He's a Spanish dancer, you know, and he's with Teresa and Luisillo. They're at the Mercury, you know, and then they're going to the South—Brighton and Bournemouth, and some other places—and after that they're taking over here while the company is abroad. By the way,' she added, 'Charles is Scottish, so he's completely the right person for James—in the ballet, *La Sylphide*, I mean. He knows how to do all the Scottish reels and strathspeys, and he's teaching me. Aren't you, Charles?'

Charles bowed slightly, but said nothing. Evidently he possessed the true Scottish gift of silence.

'And this is Rita—she's James's fiancée, Effie, in the ballet,' went on Annette, as a small fair girl with a piquant face paused at the nearest *barre* and began to practise *grands battements*. 'Wait a minute, Rita! I want to introduce you. This is Maximilian, my brother. I've been telling Max about *La Sylphide*. . . . Have you seen Hans anywhere? He's Gurn, and of course you know that Gurn is a mountaineer—in the ballet, I mean. I do think it was clever of Monsieur Georges to give Gurn to an Austrian, don't you? All Austrians are mountaineers.'

'Not Hans, my dear,' said Rita, pausing in the middle of a *battement tendu*. 'I doubt if dear Hans has even *seen* a mountain, let alone climbed one! He lived in Vienna, you know.'

'Oh, well I expect it's in his blood,' said Annette, not at all taken aback, 'even if he did live in a town.'

'Shall we rehearse *en dehors*?' said a young man who had just appeared, and now joined Rita at the nearest *barre*. 'I must say I prefer even smuts to this heat.'

'Oh, Hans!' cried Annette, 'we were just talking about you. This is Maximilian, my brother. Have you even seen a mountain, Hans?'

'Only in a picture, *petite*,' answered Hans, clicking his heels together and making a slight bow in Maximilian's direction.

'Oh, dear! And you've never climbed one then, I suppose?' said Annette with a sigh. 'Then Rita was right. It's such a disappointment. I was *sure* you would have climbed *one* mountain at least.'

'The only climbing I have ever done is up to the seventh storey of the block of flats where my parents live,' laughed Hans. 'And that only when the lift is out of order!'

After they had warmed up they went out on to the flat roof, and the rehearsal began. Someone produced an old packing-case, and Charles reclined upon it as gracefully as he could, only giving an occasional groan when a nail or a sharp corner stuck into him. La Sylphide, the temperamental Simonetta, appeared, strolling leisurely out of the dressing-room, just as Madame Boccaccio arrived, and proceeded languidly to charm the sleeping Highlander

*"They're beginning the second act."*

(Charles on his packing-case). As Annette whispered to Maximilian, it was hard to imagine so virile a Scotsman being charmed by such a lackadaisical sprite! 'In fact, she couldn't care less!' she added in an undertone.

Almost everyone has seen the lovely ballet *Les Sylphides*, but few know, or have seen, the much older *La Sylphide*, which was the first ballet in which the now well-known white tarlatan dresses were worn. *La Sylphide* was the first romantic ballet ever to be performed, and it set the fashion for romanticism, so that white tarlatan, tulle, gauze and misty effects in general became *de rigueur* in all the ballets at that time, which was about 1832. *Ballet blanc* became the rage. Marie Taglioni created the romantic rôle of La Sylphide, the spirit of the Scottish woodland and glen, who by her wiles charmed the sleeping Highlander, James, and enticed him away from the homely Effie, his betrothed, the night before their wedding.

'I don't believe she's thinking the least bit about what she's doing,' whispered Annette to Max as they waited, leaning against the grimy parapet, for the second act to begin (where the *corps de ballet* of sylphs enter). 'Monsieur Georges told her to sink down on one knee like *this*.' She noiselessly demonstrated the movement. 'He'd be furious if he were here and saw Simonetta doing an *arabesque penchée*, but I don't believe Madame Boccaccio knows it's wrong. She only knows the Petit choreography.'

'Look out!' warned Maximilian. 'They're beginning the second act. Shouldn't you be over there, *ma chère*?'

'Gosh, so I should!' exclaimed Annette, joining the rest of her sylph companions with a skip and a jump—quite unorthodox, it may be said. 'What a good thing you noticed!'

Hour after hour the ballet rehearsed, till the sun began to go down, the typists covered up their machines and went home, and the sculptor put the finishing touches to a female arm, raised—yes, in the graceful attitude of a sylph! The next day he was to wonder what exactly had made him get that effect! The distant roar of London's traffic changed to a higher note, as the rush-hour gave place to the lull before the theatres took over.

Weary but happy, Annette accompanied Maximilian down the endless flights of stairs to the bus.

'I'm afraid I can't ask you home to the convent,' she
48

explained, as they crossed the landing on the sixth flight. 'They're all nuns, you know, and they'd have a fit if I produced *you*, Max!'

'Why not come back to my digs?' said Max, as they racketed down to the fifth landing. 'My "spot" isn't till nine-thirty, and the other thing I'm in is after that, so I needn't be at the theatre till about eight, or even half past. It's only seven now.'

'Oh, that would be lovely,' said Annette. 'I'd miss tepid fish—they always have it on Fridays.' She stopped suddenly. They had come to the landing on the fourth flight. 'You see that passage? Well, if you go down there, you can get into the theatre. Like to see it?'

Max nodded, and the two of them stole down a maze of passages and galleries, and eventually found themselves outside the boxes, high above the stage in the Upper Circle. Already there was a soft glow of light in the theatre, and usherettes were preparing for the evening performance.

'There's someone down there,' said Maximilian, craning over the velvet ledge of the box nearest to him. 'Look—on the stage. It's that Simonetta girl. *Mon dieu!* but she is a beautiful dancer!'

Annette said nothing for a moment. She stood silently watching the tiny figure far, far below them. Then she said, 'You're right, Maxie—she *is* a wonderful dancer. I had no idea she could dance like that. Oh, lovely, lovely!' The Italian girl had just finished a series of dazzling turns, *pirouettes* and *fouettés*. 'That's the Odile *solo* from *Lac*, you know. Oh, she's finished!' She gave a little sigh of disappoinment. 'I thought for the moment she was going to do the Odette *solo*, too. I expect there wasn't time before the company want the stage for warming up. I wonder why she never dances like that for us?'

'Thinks herself a cut above a mere school, I expect. Come to think of it, she *does* seem a bit advanced for a ballet-school.'

'Oh, she's only in it for a few months,' Annette told him. 'She's joining the company, you know, after Christmas, and she's only with us to learn Monsieur Georges's queer ways. On this tour she is a sort of guest artist. But I expect you're right, Max, and she doesn't think we're worth the trouble of dancing for.'

.     .     .     .     .

That night Annette stood at the back of the Mercury Theatre and watched Maximilian in his 'spot'. It was a *zapateado*, and he was partnered by a vivacious dark girl whose scarlet many-flounced petticoats filled the stage with colour and a soft hissing noise as she swung them about her. The metallic click of the castenets and the thunder of Max's *zapateado*, echoed by his partner's softer beats, brought a roar of applause from the experts massed in the gallery.

'That dancer will get to the top, and quickly, I prophesy it,' said a young man with a beard and a flowing necktie— an Art student, to all appearances. 'It's queer, isn't it, how no English dancers manage to capture the true Spanish fire? Ever seen Sadler's Wells do *Tricorne*? Not up to this. . . .'

His companion, a pretty fair girl, with hair cut like a man, and scarlet slacks, agreed, and Annette smiled. She didn't undeceive them. After all, Max *wasn't* wholly English, even if he hadn't a single drop of Spanish blood in his veins!

She waited for her brother at the stage door, and the two of them caught a bus to Annette's Convent Home. Max had insisted on accompanying her, although she had assured him that she was quite used to being out in the London streets and was perfectly able to take care of herself.

'Goodbye, Maxie,' she said when they reached the steps of the tall Convent Home. 'I think you've improved enormously, and you're going to be famous in no time. I feel it in my bones.'

'Goodbye, Annette,' said Max in his turn. 'I may not see you again before I go—we're off to Brighton on Sunday early, you know. If I don't, good luck for the tour! Not that I need worry. You always did have what I call Dancer's Luck.'

'I believe you're right,' Annette said complacently as the door was opened by a round-faced nun, who was evidently on 'door duty'. 'Goodbye again, darling Max. I wish— oh. I do wish you'd been here a bit sooner. I've been so lonely. But never mind, it's been lovely just seeing you today, and we'll be off ourselves on Sunday too. It's the dress-rehearsal tomorrow. *Au revoir*, Maxie!'

'*Adios*, Annette,' said Max. And then the door closed,

and he saw the light of Annette's pocket-torch mounting the many flights of stairs to the tiny room at the top of the tall building. The electric light was all turned off at ten o'clock, Annette had explained, so, if you went in after that, you had to use a torch.

Maximilian walked slowly away and down into the Tube. There were still crowds of people everywhere. Only eleven o'clock! The night had just begun for Londoners. Yet at this self-same moment, under this same yellow moon that was quite eclipsed here in London by the dazzling neon lights, lay Castle Airdrochan, silent and asleep in the shadow of mighty Blaven. The last oil-lamp (the one in Mamie Slaughter's bedroom) had gone out, and there was no sound except the far-away roar of the waterfall in Coire Uaigneich. Strangely enough it was exactly the same sound as that of the distant London traffic that Annette could hear as she tumbled wearily into her hard little bed in the Convent Home, and fell asleep almost before her head touched the pillow.

## On Tour

THERE'S nothing like a provincial tour for educating young dancers. They performed in all sorts of places. In big theatres of industrial towns, where the wide stages had a tremendous 'rake', and the auditoriums were filled with cheering, clapping, cat-calling people. In small town halls in front of ultra-genteel audiences who clapped politely in all the correct places, and nearly froze the company with their icy reserve. They danced in theatres with great dusty velvet curtains decorated with cupids and roses, and auditoriums flanked with pillars, and dressing-rooms still alive with the ghosts of long-dead music-hall stars. In modern repertory theatres, all pale wood and tubular seats, and curtains that slid silently together revealing a futuristic design of circles and cubes. Sometimes they danced in lecture-halls with no curtains at all, merely an arrangement of screens, and nowhere to dress in except a bit of the hall roped off! They once even danced in a swimming-bath, with a stage built over the pool itself! Usually the theatres and the halls were full to capacity, because industrial England is fond of dancing of any sort (and ballet in particular), but occasionally they danced to an almost empty house—just a few rows of people in the stalls, and a large empty void behind, and a meagre scattering of people in the circles above.

Unconsciously Annette learnt many valuable lessons on this tour. How to bring out the best points of her dancing; how to cover up the bad ones; how to hide mistakes. She learnt that, nine times out of ten, the audience will not notice even the most glaring error that sets the whole company in a twitter, always provided the dancer goes on dancing as if nothing had happened. She learnt that you could even fall down right in the middle of a *pirouette* and make a joke of it. In fact you could make it an asset, because the audience felt you were human, after all, and loved you for it. In short, she learnt stage-craft, which is an even more valuable possession to a dancer than actual technique. Lots of dancers have succeeded despite weak technique, whereas other stronger dancers have remained in the *corps de ballet* because they lacked that 'sense of the theatre'.

How Annette loved it! Yes, even the endless railway journeys, sometimes lasting half the night and ending up on a draughty station platform at three in the morning! The endless changes of cheap theatrical lodgings; the irregular hours; the snatched meals eaten standing up in dressing-rooms, in station waiting-rooms, sometimes even while hurrying for a bus. Added to all this was the nervous strain: 'Will I be good enough to dance the Sugar Plum Fairy *solo* at today's matinée—my very first time?—Will I be able to turn those *fouettés en place* correctly, or will I wander away to one side of the stage, ending up nearly in the wings, and be disgraced for ever?—Will Maurice lift me at the exact split second in the Odette *solo*, and lower me so that I can sway in time with the music—that beautiful movement—or will he be just a second too late and spoil the whole *pas de deux*?—Will Philip catch me in the fish dive in *Casse Noisette*? Will he . . .?' Oh, the anxieties and worries that beset a dancer on her first tour!

Yet she loved every minute of it, despite the fact that

she worked so hard at classes and rehearsals that all she saw of the towns they visited was the theatre and the railway station! On her free day she was too tired to go out sight-seeing. All she wanted to do was to go to bed and have a real lie-in. Besides, there was the inevitable washing and darning of tights, and one's undies to keep sweet and clean. No-one is more fastidious than your professional dancer. Thank goodness, thought Annette, for nylon! Most people have reason to be grateful to scientists for producing that useful fabric, but none more so than the ballet dancers in their never-ending rush from place to place, their need for several changes of clothing each day. How wonderful to be able to strip off dripping undergarments, knowing that they could be rinsed through and dried in an hour or while one slept, and not even need ironing.

Besides loving the actual tour, Annette had another reason for feeling especially happy just now. She was getting nearer to her own beloved home. When they left the rainy Lancashire cotton towns behind, and sped across Yorkshire, with its miles and miles of rough limestone walls and its sheep, and she saw Durham cathedral perched up on its hill, she felt that Northumberland was just round the corner. Only one more town—Sunderland, at the mouth of the Wear—and she would be there! That night in her new digs she lay listening to the noises of the busy seaport —the hooting of steamers and fog-horns, the whine of cranes, the clank of machinery, and the cry of the seagulls —and thought of her home, Dancing Peel, and all the people she would meet in a short week's time. She would be dancing in a real theatre—even if it was only a small repertory one—in her home town of Newcastle. They would all come to see her dance (they'd promised)—her mother, Aunt Molly, Mr MacCrimmon, the vicar of Mintlaw, the tiny village where she lived, and perhaps Angus, his son, if he was at home. Even Bella Muckle, who 'did' for them at the Peel had promised to 'gan and see Annette dee her bit dance.' Miss Winterburn, who produced the Women's Institute plays, had said she'd be there too. Then there was a chance—just a chance, mind you—that she might get a *solo* at a *matinée*. Oh, the wonders that lay in front of little Annette Dancy! Why, the whole glittering world lay before her, waiting to be conquered. It was springtime for Annette. The dew wasn't off the wild-roses for her!

They travelled from Sunderland to Newcastle on the Sunday, so as to be ready to open on the Monday night. Annette could hardly sit still in the railway carriage, she was so excited. A helpful young soldier had got her suitcase down from the rack for her, her gloves were on, her coat was over her arm. She was all ready to spring from the train the very minute it drew alongside the platform. Why, oh why, should it stop outside Gateshead? Here was the well-known bridge across the murky Tyne, with the High Level and the Swing Bridge over to the right. She could see the cathedral-church of St Nicholas, with its famous lantern-tower. Between her and the station lay a gleaming expanse of criss-cross rails—the great railway junction. Annette felt like jumping out of the carriage, and running over the bridge on foot. Ah, they were off again! The train sidled forward for a short way, only to stop once more with a soft but firm jolt, right in the middle of the bridge! Oh, cruel train! It was doing it on purpose. It knew perfectly well that Annette Dancy was there at the carriage window, craning her neck to see round the bend into the dark familiar station on the other side. It was teasing her. So near and yet so far! It would never, never start again. . . . Ah, now it was moving slowly—but backwards!

'It's going back to Sunderland,' said Annette in despair. Then, when all hope had been given up, the direction was reversed, and the train slid softly into Newcastle Central Station. . . .

Mrs Dancy, waiting at the barrier, saw Annette when she was a long way off, and her heart leapt. When Annette had lived at home, Mrs. Dancy was too used to seeing her to notice her daughter's lovely grace, but now she saw with the eyes of a stranger the beautiful poise of the head, the way she ran forward as if she was blown by the wind, with a cry of, 'Mummy! Oh, Mummy, it's lovely to see you again!'

The young soldier (he was an American) put down Annette's case at Mrs Dancy's feet, and saluted.

'Good-day, ma'am! You've sure got a grand kid there! Goodbye, honey!' He nodded at Annette, and disappeared.

'Oh, Pete . . .' began Annette, disengaging herself from

her mother's arms. 'I haven't thanked him properly, and he's gone. He was ever so nice and helpful, Mummy. He insisted on carrying my case.' Then she saw the two figures standing a little way behind her mother.

'Angus!' she cried. 'And Mr MacCrimmon! How lovely of you both to come and meet me. Isn't it sweet of them, Mummy?'

'It was a pleasure,' said Angus with a little bow. If Annette hadn't been so excited, or so much taken up with greeting her mother, she would have noticed the glow that came into his blue eyes when he beheld her, but she was far too busy looking around her at the well-known station, and all the familiar landmarks. In the vicar's car they sped up Grainger Street, and there, on his column, stood Earl Grey, looking down on the city he had helped to build. And there were all the shops she knew, looking very small after the big London ones, but very smart for all that. Annette loved them all.

They had tea at a café in Blackett Street before going home to Aunt Molly's flat, and while they ate, they talked. It was mostly Annette who did the talking. She had to tell them all about the tour—what towns they had visited, and how she would get a whole fortnight's holiday at the end of the tour. They had to hear how Simonetta had developed a cold ('though I think she made it up really') and couldn't dance the Sugar Plum Fairy *solo*, so Paddy had done it in the evenings, and Annette in the *matinées*, because she and Paddy were the only ones who had good enough figures to stand the classical costume, Annette told them complacently. As we have said before, modesty in regard to her dancing was not Annette's strong point. 'And they say she isn't going to be well enough to dance in Newcastle either,' she went on. 'Simonetta, I mean. So that means we won't be doing *La Sylphide*, because Simonetta's the only one who Monsieur Georges thinks can dance the leading rôle. We all think that Simonetta considers herself above provincial audiences, but wait till we get to Edinburgh, and Monsieur Georges joins us. She'll perk up and be on stage all the time everyone says! But what do I care, as long as I can dance in Newcastle. . . . Oh, and guess what? Do you know where we're having our morning classes, and doing our rehearsing while we're here? Yes, at dear old Nellie Brandon's! I can hardly believe it! What a thrill to be going back to one's old dancing-school as a—well, I suppose you could almost call me a *ballerina*,' said Annette with a proud toss of her hand, 'when I'm doing the Sugar Plum Fairy. Anyway, I'm a professional dancer. Oh, yes—we get paid while we're on this tour. Of course it only amounts to pocket-money, but it's useful for make-up and so forth. . . .'

On and on she talked, and never noticed the attention she was receiving from the people sitting at the tables all around. Her vivacious little face (even if it *was* plain) with its luminous eyes, now flashing, now soft as dark-brown velvet, reflecting every emotion; her lovely expressive hands, her grace. Oh, it was obvious to the most casual onlooker that here was no ordinary little girl. Even the waitresses were fascinated, and the conductor of the string orchestra struck up *Alice Blue Gown*, because the little girl at the corner table was wearing blue! Angus, sitting opposite her, thought she was even more attractive than he remembered her, yet, at the same time, she hadn't changed a bit!

The weeks flew by, and in no time at all the *matinée* at which Annette was to dance the Sugar Plum Fairy (yes, fortunately Simonetta's cold had persisted) arrived. They all came to see her—a whole row of them in the best seats. When she finished the dance with a splendid flourish, as if to say, 'Aren't I beautiful?' (which she was), they all clapped their hands sore, and all the people sitting near clapped too, and hoped for an *encore*, not knowing that there are no *encores* in a ballet performance.

After the show, they all went back-stage, and were duly awestruck at the sight of Annette and all the other dancers, complete with make-up, strolling in and out of the dressing-rooms and on the now darkened stage, talking 'shop'. They were all very young, these dancers, their average age being about eighteen, but, listening to them, you might have imagined yourself back-stage at Covent Garden. No-one could have said that these young people didn't take their Art seriously. Each dance was discussed, and pulled to pieces, and they criticised each other's appearance quite candidly. . . . 'Annette, *chérie*, you 'ave too much of ze shadow on ze eyes. Too long of ze eyelash! On Covent Garden stage, 'alf a mile or so away from ze audience, *oui*,

56

*oui, oui*! *Ça va*! but in zis leetle theatre, it make ze eyes look 'alf shut—as if you go about in a dream, hey! You should take ze lines so, and *so*.' Marie, a French dancer, demonstrated her skill upon Annette's face, drawing swift skilful lines of grease-paint at the corners of the eyes, and then standing back at a little distance to view her handiwork. *'Ça va mieux, oui?'* 'Oh, *no*, Marie. That makes her look far too sophisticated. It should be like this,' put in Paddy, Annette's Irish friend. 'Don't you think so, Mrs Dancy?' Annette's mother wanted to say that she preferred her daughter with no make-up on at all, but she was far too wise.

'I think I agree, Paddy,' she said, choosing the lesser of two evils.

Annette studied her reflection earnestly in her make-up mirror.

'I think Marie is right,' she said at length. 'At least, so far. The lines, but no false eyelashes. I'll try it that way next time. Thanks, Marie! . . . Well, I'm going home now —I mean, really home, to Dancing Peel. Good-bye, every one. I'm not on tonight. Best of luck!'

'Good-bye!' *'Au revoir!' 'Adios!'* ' 'Bye, sweet! Here's hoping you have a lovely time!' *'A bientôt*, Annette, *chérie*. Our love to the Peel.' (Oh, yes, they had all heard about Annette's historic home!) *'Adios*, Annette!' Their voices, British and foreign, followed her out of the dressing-room, and down the stairs to the waiting car (Mr MacCrimmon's car).

'Aren't they sweet? Aren't I lucky?' said Annette as she squeezed herself into the back seat next to Angus, and they drove away. 'I adore every one of them—except Simonetta,' she amended. 'Simonetta is my rival!'

'OH, the darling Peel!' cried Annette, hanging perilously out of the car window, as the rugged old building came into view from behind a belt of fir trees. 'You haven't changed a bit!'

'You didn't expect it to have grown a stucco façade, or sprouted little balconies, did you?' laughed the vicar. 'No, I think that old peel will stay just as it is until it falls down —which will be a very long time, by the look of it. I don't imagine any of us will be here to see the sad day.'

He was right. Architects might divide the peel inside into nice tidy modern flats; they might push doors through the six-foot-thick walls, they might add a staircase, where before was only a ladder, they might convert an ancient storeroom into a modern bathroom. They might even put in electric light (though as yet there were no signs of that!). But whatever they did inside, outside, the old peel-tower remained unscathed. Sombre dignified old Border fortress! —it would take more than a mere diocesan architect to change Dancing Peel.

'How lovely to have a whole evening at home, and nothing at all to do but talk,' Annette said, when they reached the lodge in the drive where they were to stay for the week-end.

Mrs Dancy looked very guilty.

'What's the matter, Mummy? Why are you looking like that?' demanded Annette, who knew her mother's every mood.

'Well, as a matter of fact, darling, the village has arranged a barn dance tonight especially in your honour, and they told me that everyone was hoping you'd dance at it—ballet, I mean.'

Annette opened her mouth to exclaim, 'Botheration! Why can't people leave me alone for just one night?' Then she shut it again. Here was one of the obligations of her chosen career—to be always ready and happy to entertain and entrance people with her Art when it was convenient to her, and when it wasn't. She was often to think of this

58

in later days when she had to stay behind in her dressing-room or at the stage-door signing autographs on bits of paper, answering stupid questions, when all she wanted to do was to go home to bed.

'Oh, well—I shall still have all tomorrow,' she said; 'at least, nearly all. I have to be back in Newcastle by six. I can go to church in the morning, and spend the rest of the time looking round the dear old peel, and visiting in the village. . . . Oh, but, Mummy, I've just thought of an awful thing—I haven't anything to dance in. I mean a costume.'

"All your dancing clothes are here—just as you left them,' said Mrs Dancy with a smile. She didn't tell Annette the number of hours she had spent washing and mending them, and putting them away in layers of tissue paper. 'They will need to be ironed a little, to get out the creases, that's all.'

So here was Annette at the ironing-board again, just as she had been a year ago. It was as if the last year had never been, thought Angus, as he watched her delicate fingers flying in and out of the crushed net, coaxing the frills into place, and pressing them down dexterously with the warm iron.

'What are you dancing tonight?' he asked her. 'Or haven't you decided yet?'

'Well, it will have to be something with a long Sylphide dress,' answered Annette, looking out at him from underneath a thick mist of diaphanous net skirts, 'because my *tutu* is beyond repair. The trouble is I did the Waltz from *Les Sylphides* last time, at the Women's Institute Concert. I don't expect they'd remember it, but you never know—Miss Winterburn might. She knows quite a lot about ballet. I think I shall do the *solo* in the first act of our new ballet, *La Sylphide*. That's the one where the sylph charms the Highlander, James, as he lies asleep in the farmhouse, you know.'

Angus didn't know, but he nodded.

'Go on,' he said. 'Tell me about it.'

'Well, as I was saying,' went on Annette, 'James is asleep. I think it would be an awfully good idea if *you* were James, Angus,'

Poor Angus blushed.

'You—you mean in your ballet, Annette?'

59

'Yes, in my ballet, of course. You'd be asleep, so all you would have to do would be to lie in a chair with your eyes shut, and then, right at the end of my dance, you'd wake up and see me.'

'No,' said Angus firmly. 'I do not think that would be a good idea at all. I am doing many things for you, Annette, but become a ballet-dancer for you I will not.'

'Oh, all right,' she answered. 'I didn't think you would, really. Well, I shall just have to ask the audience to *pretend* James is there.'

'That will be a much better idea,' said Angus with relief. Really, one never knew what outrageous thing Annette would suggest next!

When Annette saw the elaborate preparations that had been made in her honour, she felt ashamed at having thought, even for a moment, that it was a nuisance to dance at the village barn dance. They couldn't have taken more trouble if she had been Margot Fonteyn herself! The supper was arranged on long trestle-tables in the schoolroom, and everyone from miles around had brought contributions. There were mountains of Sally Muirhead's dropped-scones, thickly plastered with deep yellow farm butter, and on either side was a phalanx of 'singing-hinnies' (as girdle-scones are called in Northumberland), mincepies (Mintlaw didn't keep them only for Christmas) and sausage-rolls, filled with home-grown sausage, as Annette put it. These were to be 'hotted up' at the last minute by old Sally herself, who boiled the water on the big open fire in two kettles, black as witches' cauldrons. Down the middle of the tables, with the pollen of the meadowsweet and meadow-cranesbill dropping upon them, were cakes 'of the most exquisite', as Maximilian would have said had he seen them—cakes filled with whipped cream, and, as if that wasn't enough, more cream laid on in dollops on top of the icing. There were chocolate cakes that melted in the mouth, sandwich-cakes oozing jam made of raspberries gathered in the little cottage gardens, or wild strawberries out of the woods. There were plates of granny-loaf, made with milk, and a pile of Hannah Dobson's famous rock-cakes, mixed with cream.

'Oh, I simply must pinch just one now!' exclaimed Annette when she saw them. 'I know I'm nearly sixteen and practically grown up, but I just can't resist Hannah's "rockies".'

There were trifles too, carefully covered with snowy napkins to keep them hidden from the gleaming amber eyes of Sally's Timmy. Last Harvest Home, Timmy had demolished most of the cream off the top of the trifles while Sally's back was turned. She had taught her kitten to do it too, and now here they both were, rubbing themselves against the legs of the tables and trying to look very innocent. Incidentally Timmy's kitten had grown into a great velvety black tom, with a deep melodious voice, and a strong back that arched like a bow when you stroked him. He had been named Sheba originally, but when she had discovered his sex Annette had rechristened him Black Lad (after Angus's famous piper ancestor) before she went to London; but although old Sally tried hard to use this high-sounding name, it was usually shortened to Blackie.

Right in the middle of the longest table was a large fruit-cake, iced with white and pink, and in the middle, posed *en arabesque*, was a ballet-dancer, cunningly fashioned of wire, with net skirts and a tiny ball of cotton-wool for a head.

'Oh, how lovely! I wonder who made it?' exclaimed Annette in delight when she saw it.

'Our George made un,' said Mary Sowerby, the blacksmith's wife, and George's mother, proudly. 'Right handy is our George.'

'Well, I think it's wonderful,' said Annette. 'Will you thank him for me very much, Mrs Sowerby. . . . Oh, it's all right—there he is! I can thank him myself.'

She made her way through the crowds of people to the far side of the room, where George lounged with his cronies. He was close on six feet tall, and he positively towered over Annette, though he wasn't more than a year older than she.

'Thank you for making me the lovely dancer, George,' she said when she reached him. 'I think it's just perfect.'

'I was pleased to dee it, Miss Annette,' said George, shifting uncomfortably from one foot to the other and turning very red in the face. He felt that the little girl he had known all his life had grown up. She might be as tiny as a fairy, but there was a certain dignity about her that made him suddenly tongue-tied. 'You're very welcome,' was all he could say.

Annette's dance was at half past ten (they'd left it late, so that everyone should be there to see her). When she came out of the ladies' cloak-room in her floating net dress there was a burst of clapping. She had borrowed a tartan scarf from Martha Keenliside, and fastened it on one shoulder with a huge cairngorm brooch belonging to Bella Muckle. On her dark hair rested a tiny wreath of starry white flowers. Actually they were dog-daisies, and just an hour ago they'd been growing in the Long Meadow behind Sarah Dodd's cottage. With Angus's help she had fashioned two tiny wings out of scraps of net and wire. As she hadn't the proper Loevenskjold music, she had altered the dance a little, so that she could use an arrangement of Chopin. It was played on the school piano (moved into the village hall for the occasion) by the organist, paler and longer-haired than ever now that his choir had won a medal at the Northumbrian Music Festival!

After her dance was over, and she had graciously acknowledged all the compliments that were showered upon her, Annette strolled out on to the village green with Angus at her side. She was still in her white floating dress, and the moon, hanging in the dark-blue evening sky like a great golden lantern, shone through the misty folds of net and made her look like a sylph indeed.

'Let's go into the peel,' she said to Angus. 'Although I know the alterations aren't finished, I can't go away without paying it a visit—even though I'm coming back again in a few weeks' time.'

She did not notice that Angus said nothing to this. But as a matter of fact Angus very often said nothing. He was content to watch Annette and let her do the chattering.

'I know we shall have to be careful where we walk,' she went on as they crossed the dewy grass and let themselves into the old building. 'Mummy says that some of the floor boards are up in the Round Lounge and the staircase is being altered.'

'We will go up the old stone one,' said Angus, 'and so out on to the roof—if that will be pleasing you, Annette.' He led the way, shining the torch so that she shouldn't trip over the piles of workmen's tools and loose floor boards that were lying about everywhere.

'Oh, I simply must look into my own little bedroom!' she cried, when they reached the top of the spiral staircase and Angus was about to unbolt the door at the bottom of the still steeper stairway leading out on to the flat roof of the peel. 'It's funny to think that I shall be sleeping in it again in just a few weeks' time.'

Again Angus was silent.

'It does seem an awful long way off being finished,' she observed, as they peeped into the well-known room. 'Why, the floor's still up!' She tiptoed across the floor to the window, balancing precariously on the rafters (it was like walking on stepping-stones!) 'You'd never think they'd get it finished in time for my holidays.'

'Annette,' Angus began, 'there is something I must tell you—something your mother asked me to tell you——'

'Mummy?' said Annette in surprise. 'Why ever should Mummy ask *you* to tell me anything, Angus? I should have thought she'd have told me herself. How queer of her! What is it, Angus?' She leaned her thin white arms on the stone window-sill, and pressed her cheek against the rough stones, loving the feel of them.

Angus cleared his throat.

'I am trying to tell you, Annette—trying to tell you——'

'Well, go on, then—tell me,' said Annette impatiently. 'What's the matter with you, Angus?' Then, at last, the truth dawned on her. 'Angus—you're not, you're *not* going to tell me it *won't* be finished in time for my holidays? You mustn't say that! I couldn't bear it!'

'I am afraid that it is so,' said Angus gravely.

'You mean—not only my bedroom, but the whole peel? You mean that we shan't be able to live here at all?' Annette said, unable to believe that such a tragedy could happen.

Angus nodded.

'Then, I suppose we shall just have to live in your lodge,' said Annette, not very politely, it must be admitted, since it was very kind of the vicar to house them in his cottage anyway.

'I am afraid that that is not possible either,' answered Angus. 'You see, Annette, the lodge has been let from next week, and the new people will be living there.'

63

'And your father?'

'He will be taking his holiday then, so he will not be needing to live at Mintlaw. He will be at Portree in the Island of Skye.'

'And you, Angus?'

'I shall be spending the last weeks of my holidays on the Island also,' said Angus. 'But not at Portree. I shall be staying with my friend Gordon of Airdrochnish at his home, and we shall be climbing together in the Black Cuillin. That will be fine, of course, but'—his face clouded—'it will mean that I shall not be seeing you, Annette.'

They had come out on to the flat roof by this time, and Annette's eyes were all for the wild expanse of Border moorland spread out before her, so that she did not notice the shadow in his eyes. All she saw were the fronds of bracken, silvered by the bright moonlight, and the glint of the Mintlaw Burn flowing amongst its rushes. There was no sound except the cry of a late-flying curlew, and the skirl of Jack Armstrong's pipes when someone opened the door of the village hall to get a breath of fresh air.

Angus looked down at Annette, standing there in all her lovely grace, and knew that he had fallen in love with her. Of course he might never marry her (who knew what the future might hold for either of them?), but he would never forget her as she stood there, the moon shining on her daisy wreath, and her dress blowing in the night wind. He was only seventeen—far too young to fall in love according to the standards of the modern world, yet he loved Annette truly. Poor Angus! First love is a painful thing, no less painful because grown-up people do not take it seriously. As for Annette, she was very young for her age, and wholly taken up with her dancing. She was quite unaware of the fact that she had awakened this boy's love. All her heart was given to her profession, and if there *was* a tiny corner left over, it was for her mother and her beloved Border home. Therefore what came next was a shock to her, so you must forgive her if she didn't behave either very kindly, or with much imagination.

'You are knowing that it is my birthday tomorrow,' Angus said, his language becoming very stilted, as it always did when he was feeling any strong emotion. 'I very well remember my last one. I spent it looking for you, Annette, in the Keilder Forest!'

'Oh, Angus, so you did!' cried Annette, conscience-stricken. 'I forgot all about it. I'm so sorry, I haven't even got a present for you, and tomorrow's Sunday. Why didn't you remind me?'

'It is of no account,' said Angus gravely.

'Oh, but it *is*, it *is*!' insisted Annette. 'I wouldn't have had it happen for the world. What would you like for a present, Angus? I have lots of money now, you know. I can give you anything you like—unless you choose something for hunting,' she added firmly. 'I positively refuse to give you anything for hunting. You know how much I detest chasing things.'

'What could you give me that would be for hunting?' asked Angus curiously.

'Oh, I don't know.' Annette wracked her brains. 'A tail-bandage for your horse, perhaps, or—or a hoof-pick, or a riding-crop. Of course if you promised solemnly not to use it for hunting—the tail-bandage, I mean——'

'I am not wanting a tail-bandage for my horse, nor a hoof-pick, nor even a riding-crop,' interposed Angus with a little smile. Annette was really very funny when she was serious!

'Oh, then you do want *something*,' said Annette, with a sigh of relief. 'That's a blessing anyhow, because I can't think of anything else. What is it you want, Angus? It doesn't matter how much it costs.'

'What I am wanting does not cost anything at all— I mean in money,' the boy told her. 'It is this.' Before she knew what he was about, he had put both hands on her shoulders and kissed her upturned lips.

Annette was so surprised that for a moment she did nothing at all. Then she tore herself free, and slapped him hard, first on one cheek and then on the other.

'How dare you! How dare you! I shall never forgive you, never! I shall never speak to you again!'

She rushed off down the little staircase, leaving Angus standing there. Half way down, she paused. After all, he hadn't done anything very dreadful, had he, even if it *was* unexpected? It wasn't as if he'd been hunting a fox. Besides, she'd asked him what he wanted for his birthday, so she was really herself to blame, for being so stupid. Her heart began to bleed for him. Oh, poor, poor Angus! (Besides, her precious ankles; she was in danger of twisting

65

them on the dark stairway.) She rushed back again, and arrived on the roof, panting.

'Angus . . .'

He was still standing where she had left him.

'Annette?'

'Although you shouldn't have done what you did, I oughtn't to have slapped you,' said Annette. 'It was most unladylike, and I'm very sorry. Please forgive me.'

'There is nothing to forgive,' said Angus stiffly. He looked so tall and forbidding that she began to be afraid of him. However, she screwed up her courage and advanced towards him.

'You can kiss me again, if you like,' she offered. 'And I won't slap you—I promise.'

'Thank you, Annette, but I am not wanting to kiss you now.'

'Oh, please—just to show that you've forgiven me.'

If Angus hadn't been feeling so hurt and sad, he might have laughed at the sight of Annette standing there, face upraised, eyes tightly shut. As it was he stood there silently.

Annette opened her eyes again.

'I do wish you'd *say* something, Angus!' she exclaimed. 'I wish you wouldn't just stand there saying nothing.'

'There is nothing to say.'

'Well, you can say "I forgive you, Annette" for a beginning,' prompted Annette.

'I am forgiving you, Annette,' repeated Angus. 'Will that content you?'

Suddenly Annette lost her patience.

'Angus Alexander MacCrimmon!' she exclaimed. 'You always *were* the most aggravating boy alive!' Then she stood on the extreme tips of her toes, pulled his head down towards her, and kissed him tenderly: '*There!* Will that do? Now we're friends?'

Angus had to laugh.

'Annette, you are the funniest wee lassie,' he said in his turn. 'But yes, we are friends, and I promise you that I will not offend again.'

I T was in Edinburgh that the dramatic thing happened, which is quite natural, when you come to think of it, since Edinburgh is a dramatic city. In fact, it is a theatrical city, with its back-cloth of mountains, and its historic Royal Mile, climbing, higgledy-piggledy, up to its fairytale castle in the clouds. Moreover, Monsieur Georges joined them at Edinburgh. Everything was set for drama!

Simonetta was at her best, dazzling the audience with her brilliance, until they began to whisper things about a 'second Fonteyn'. *La Sylphide* was well received by the Edinburgh audience. It was a ballet after their own hearts; indeed, it might have been made for them, and the girl who danced the main rôle was full of fire. 'But she shouldn't be full of fire,' did I hear someone say? 'She should be dreamy and fey.'

'Och, mon, but I am liking a little of the fireworks masel'. Are there ony seats left for tonight? No? Weel, more's the pity. I should hae liked fine to see yon lassie again.'

Yes, they were a great success, especially Simonetta. The papers were full of her, and all sang her praises. Annette, watching her from the wings, was so fascinated by her daring innovations (the brazen way she was changing the choreography to suit her own style, and achieving a personal success at the expense of the ballet) that several times she completely forgot her own small parts and came in late. Once she forgot to come in at all!

'Oh, well, it doesn't really matter,' she thought. 'The audience doesn't notice a sylph or two less. They certainly wouldn't miss *me*!'

As for Monsieur Georges, he positively glowered as he stood in the wings watching Simonetta 'putting across' all the De Cuevas tricks (as he called them), and ignoring his, Georges Reinholt Dutoit's, choreography. At last the bomb exploded. Simonetta excelled herself. Instead of gliding from the wings like a very sylph, and kneeling beside the sleeping James, she entered with a series of

67

brilliant turns, finishing up with a treble *pirouette* and *arabesque penchée* on the arm of the Highlander's chair. Incidentally she drew a burst of applause from the delighted audience. Monsieur Georges growled so loudly it was a wonder he wasn't heard from the auditorium. And so it went on. The last straw (if one might call it that) was the exit of La Sylphide. Simonetta was supposed to *courru* back-stage into the misty wood, her arms outstretched in a beseeching gesture, as if she were being drawn away against her will. James was to take one or two steps after her, turn and behold the wedding procession—that of his betrothed, Effie, who had, by this time, married his best man, Gurn. Instead of this touching scene Simonetta did a series of brilliant *déboués* all round the stage, and finally disappeared to a positive roar of applause from an audience completely carried away by her brilliance, an audience who neither knew nor cared that Monsieur Georges's heart was breaking in the wings—breaking because of his beautiful ballet, ruined, quite ruined by one stupid *danseuse* who was thinking only of her own dancing and not of his so-beautiful choreography.

After the performance the storm broke.

'My goodness!' exclaimed Paddy to Annette. 'Did you see Monsieur Georges's face when Simonetta did those travelling *fouettés*? It was positively livid! He's talking to her now back-stage and, by the sound, they're having a slap-up quarrel. Personally I shouldn't be the least bit surpised if she walked out on us. After all, it's obvious she doesn't care *that*'—Paddy snapped her fingers—'for the tour. The only town she considers worth dancing in is Edinburgh. Well, we're finished here tonight, and her press notices have been so wonderful she'll be able to join any company she likes. Even Sadler's Wells, I shouldn't wonder. So her best move is to stage a quarrel with Monsieur Georges.'

'But what about her contract?' demanded Annette.

'She hasn't got one,' said Paddy. 'None of us have after all, we're only a school, really, getting a bit of experience. And anyway, she's only in the school because it's a regulation that everyone has to be for a short time before they're taken into the company. Yes, our Simonetta certainly has all her buttons on, as they say!'

As usual Paddy was right. Almost before the words were

out of her mouth a summons arrived. Monsieur Georges wished to speak to the whole company on stage. So down they all went to the queer ghostly place, with its backcloth of a forest glade, and the dusty flies overhead, and its great grey curtain cutting them off from the empty auditorium.

'Madamoiselle Simonetta has decided to travel back to London first thing tomorrow morning,' said Monsieur Georges without preamble. 'She refuses to carry out my wishes, and I will not bow to hers. So'—he shrugged his shoulders expressively—'*que faire*? What ees there to do? Moreover'—his temper rose as he contemplated the mocking face of the temperamental Simonetta—'moreover *you*' —he shifted his gaze and pointed to the horror-stricken Annette—'you, who do not even know the steps of the mere *corps de ballet*—oh, yes, I have watched you from the wings on the last three nights, and nothing, nothing have you remembered—*you* can go home too. You will be good company for each other!'

He turned and stalked off the stage, leaving the company staring after him in silence.

The tears began to roll down Annette's cheeks. All was lost! She was to go home now, just when the tour was at the peak of its success.

'Well, you know you 'ave deserve eet, *chérie*,' said Marie. 'But cheer up—there are on-ly two more of the towns—Fort William and Dun-dee. Then our holiday, and after that he weel 'ave forgot. He remember things for so leetle a time, our Monsieur Georges. And after all, you do *not* know eet—confess!'

'I may not know the stupid *corps de ballet*,' sobbed Annette, 'but I know the other part. I know it backwards.'

'I suppose by "it" you mean the chief rôle, my sweet?' remarked a girl called Pandora nastily. She had always been jealous of Annette, and was now rejoicing in her downfall.

'Yes, I *do* mean the chief rôle,' flashed back Annette. 'I can dance every step of it.'

'You're telling me!' drawled Pandora.

'I *am* telling you,' said Annette. 'And if you don't believe me, watch me!' She began the *solo* for the first act —the *solo* she had done in the little village hall of Mintlaw only a few weeks ago. Since she was going home in disgrace tomorrow, she would dance her beloved Sylphide for

69

*"Annette Dancy!"* he thundered

the last time. It would be a sort of 'swan song'. When a swan knew it was going to die, it sang before its death. Well, Annette Dancy would do so now, only she would dance instead! 'Partner me, please, Charles,' she begged. 'Oh, please, *please* partner me.'

Charles (who was James) did so obligingly, and so did Hans (who was Gurn), and Rita (who was Effie). The pianists, who played for the little company on two pianos, whistled the haunting music—just to comfort the child whom they all loved (except Pandora, who had retired in high dudgeon and left them to it. What did she care about the antics of a conceited little upstart like Annette Dancy!).

So it was that Monsieur Georges, hearing the noise from the corridor outside the dressing-rooms, strode back to see what it was all about. He beheld a strange sight—the entire company dancing his ballet, *La Sylphide*, on a darkened stage, without music, and with that stupid child, Annette Dancy, whom he had had such high hopes of, but who apparently would not work and was, moreover, a complete nit-wit, dancing the leading rôle. He opened his mouth to annihilate her. Then shut it again. Why, she was dancing as he had never seen her dance before! There was no question as to whether she knew the part, or was thinking about what she was doing. She *was* La Sylphide. The strange fey atmosphere—totally lacking in Simonetta's brilliant dancing—was here now. Moreover she was doing it the way he, Georges Reinholt Dutoit, knew it should be done—an *arabesque penchée* here; a *courru* there; a weaving of the arms; *courru* again—yes, she'd got the Bournaville choreography all right! He began to smile and move his head in time with her movements. She was musical in the extreme. He'd been right. He'd known that this child had the makings of a dancer the very first time he'd seen her in her provincial dancing-school. But, of course he, Georges Reinholt Dutoit, was always right!

Near the end of the famous scene, where the sylph loses her wings and melts away into the shadowy wood, he strode out of his hiding-place.

'Annette Dancy!' he thundered.

Annette fell to earth with a crash—a real crash it was too, since she was in the middle of a 'lift'. She sank down in a curtsy before the great man and waited for the end to come.

71

'Since you have taken so much trouble to learn someone else's rôle instead of your own, you will go on dancing it —until the end of the tour,' said Monsieur Georges.

Annette looked up through her tears. She couldn't believe her ears.

'Monsieur?'

'You 'ave 'eard what I said. You are not deaf, are you? Then do it, and do not argue,' said Monsieur Georges. (As if she would!) 'But at the end of the tour, when you return to the school, you will forget that you 'ave dance a leading rôle and do some work, hey? *C'est entendu?*'

'Yes, oh, *yes*, Monsieur Georges,' said Annette with shining eyes. 'Of course I will. I'll dance in the *corps de ballet* for the rest of my life, if you'll let me do this.'

'I do not think that is likely at all,' said Monsieur Georges dryly. 'But for now I go to my bed. I am quite exhausted! *Bonsoir, mesdames! Bonsoir, messieurs!*' He made the company two stiff little bows and was gone.


## Fort William

EVERYONE had told them about Fort William. How it was situated on the shore of beautiful Loch Linnhe; how it consisted of one small street of fascinating shops, overflowing with tartans and hand-knitted garments; how, towering above it, was mighty Ben Nevis, the highest mountain in the British Isles. What they had not been told, however, was that in Fort William it rained on three hundred and twenty-seven days in the year, and that the wettest of all the wet months was August! Yes, thought Annette, as she splashed down the main street doing her shopping, living in Fort William during August was rather like living under a shower-bath with the shower turned to 'on' all the time! To be sure, it was warm rain, and nobody seemed to take the least notice of it, but still it *was* rain, and the sad fact remained that they hadn't even seen the famous Ben up to now. During the whole week he had been cut off by a thick cloud of mist, at the exact spot where the British Aluminium Company's works scar his massive flanks, and not one fleeting glimpse had they had of his august head.

Annette had walked with Paddy up a pathway where a signpost pointed saying GLEN NEVIS, which (so the soft-voiced Scotswoman in the grocery store had told them) was 'very bonny. Not that I have been there masel', mind you, but I am hearing the young men and the lassies frae the Youth Hostel talk aboot it.' But all that Paddy and Annette had seen, after an hour's wet walk, was a swirling blanket of mist in the place where they imagined the top of Ben Nevis to be. It was very disappointing.

'I think Scotland is definitely overrated,' Annette declared, as they squelched their way back to their digs, taking shelter in a shop *en route* to avoid an especially heavy shower. 'Except for Edinburgh, which was grand, I wouldn't give *that* for it.' She snapped her fingers contemptuously. 'I think it's terribly gloomy.'

Poor Annette. She was feeling gloomy herself. Things had not gone well for her so far. The company was dancing in a tiny hall on the outskirts of the little town. There were no curtains, only an arrangement of screens, and the stage creaked. This wouldn't have mattered at all, at all, as Paddy said, if it hadn't been for the sad but indisputable fact that the craze for ballet hadn't yet reached Fort William. Audiences were almost non-existent. James, asleep in his armchair, with La Sylphide (Annette, trying her best to dance charmingly, though she felt more like bursting into tears) appearing out of the shadows, failed to move them the least little bit. They preferred a good swinging eightsome reel, with a few loud Scottish 'hoochs', to these dances done in point-shoes and white dresses. No, Fort William had yet to be converted to classical ballet.

'It's all very well for the Arts Council to call us pioneers of culture,' panted Paddy, as she came off the stage and collapsed into Annette's arms. Her Sugar Plum Fairy had been received in silence, stony as only a Scottish silence can be. 'It's all very well for them. They aren't here. But it's depressing, it is. No wonder Monsieur Georges went back to London after the first gloomy night. It's a hard struggle I'm havin' to keep the Irish temper of me from flarin' up and throwing me ballet-shoes at them!'

'Well, it won't be much longer now,' answered Annette,

as she settled her wreath of white flowers in readiness for Act One of *La Sylphide*. 'This is Friday and it's our last performance here. Then tomorrow it's Dundee, and the end of the tour.' She sighed at the thought of it. The end of the tour was the end of her triumphal march, if you could call it that. Yes, it would be the last time she'd be dancing a principal rôle in any ballet for a very long time. Monsieur Georges would keep her well in the background after this. She knew he would! He'd be afraid of her becoming swollen-headed.

'Oh, but dar-leeng,' broke in French Marie. "Ave you not 'eard ze news? We go not to Dun-dee.'

'Not go to Dundee?' repeated Annette, a sick feeling coming into her heart. Surely, surely this miserable performance, with an audience of a couple of rows of unappreciative people, couldn't be her last—her very last appearance in the leading rôle. It couldn't be! Fate wouldn't be so unkind. 'But I thought it was all arranged?'

'So it was, but eet 'as been altered,' went on Marie imperturbably. 'We change our plans, *oui*. We were to go to Dun-dee. Now we go to Portree in ze island of Skye.'

'Skye?' repeated Annette stupidly.

'Oh, yes. While you and Pad-ee were out on your leetle —'ow you call 'im?—jaunt, Dun-dee 'as fall through, as you say, so now we are to go to Portree on ze Island of Skye. Eet ees quite thrilling, *n'est-ce pas?*'

Annette hadn't time to answer, because just at that moment the stage hands lifted the screens to one side and her ballet had begun. It was not until the first interval that she was able to speak to Marie again.

'You *did* say Skye, Marie?' she said, returning to the attack as they rested in the dressing-room, which was a tiny place behind the stage packed full of music-stands and bagpipes—evidently Fort William owned a pipe band which practised here. Incidentally Annette and her friends found those music-stands very useful to put their clothes on! 'I must say the Island of Skye seems a funny sort of a place for a ballet to go. Are you *quite* sure it was Skye, Marie?'

'*Mais, oui*, of course I am sure, *chérie*. We are to dance at ze Skye Gazzering——'

'She means the Skye Gathering,' interposed Helen, a

74

rather stolid fair-haired girl, useful in the *corps de ballet* for the simple reason that she never forgot anything. 'We're to dance at the ball in Portree. They're having a cabaret, and they've heard about *La Sylphide* (from the Edinburgh papers, I imagine), and they think it would suit them. Scottish flavour, and so on, with a bit of sophistication. More than half the people who go to the Skye Gathering Ball are English anyway—Londoners mostly—and they have to be catered for.'

'Oh, yes, but ze uzzer 'alf weel all be 'Ighlanders, *naturellement,*' put in Marie, giving a graphic imitation of swinging kilts and plaids, and finishing with a step or two of a Highland Fling. 'For me, I lof ze 'Ighlanders. So picturesque, eh? But as Hélène say, there weel be many uzzer people also, and a ballet ees—I cannot say eet in ze Eenglish—*de rigueur.*'

'You mean "all the thing", I expect, Marie,' laughed Annette.

'Yes—zat ees right—all ze sing. *Comme c'est drôle* ze Eengleesh language! *Enfin,* on ze morning of tomorrow we take ze train to Mallaig, and so we go across ze *mer* to ze Island of Skye.'

'Swim or fly?' asked Paddy facetiously.

'*En bateau, naturellement,*' said Marie, taking her seriously. 'How else, *chère amie*? For me, I think zat eet ees good. One evening to perform, and zen we go 'ome. One extra week of 'oliday because of ze fall through of Dun-dee. *C'est bien ça!*'

'If only—if *only* it could have been a week at Dancing Peel,' thought Annette. Still, even if she had to stay in a town flat, she would be with her darling mother, and they could at least take the bus and spend the day at Mintlaw. She felt a little cheered at the thought, especially as a crowd of people came into the hall for the last half of the programme and filled the front rows, so that at least you couldn't *see* the empty ones behind, even if you knew they were there. Fortunately Annette never found out that the newcomers were students from Glasgow University who were staying at a Holiday Camp near by, and that they'd been given free tickets and ordered to attend as part of their cultural education.

As we have said before, it had never once stopped raining all the time the dancers were at Fort William, and not once had Ben Nevis, aloof as any *prima ballerina assoluta*, condescended to show his head. And then it happened— yes, in the middle of the night, or rather, it would be more correct to say, at three o'clock in the morning. Annette, who shared a room with Paddy in the little house on the outskirts of the town, woke up to find the moon shining on her face. And there, framed in the open window (for it was a warm night) was a great mountain with a powdering of snow upon his head.

'*Paddy!*' shrieked Annette, awake in an instant. 'Wake up, Paddy! He's here! We've seen him!'

'Who is?' murmured Paddy, still half asleep. 'W-what's the matter? It's never time to get up. Sure, an' we've only just this minute gone to bed, so we have.'

'It's Ben Nevis!' said Annette, leaping out of bed. 'Come and look at him, Paddy, me darlint! We may never see him again. Oh, the beautiful, beautiful mountain!'

'He looks on the bulky side,' said Paddy, rubbing her eyes. 'Still, he's big all right, and it's stopped raining.'

'So it has,' said Annette. 'I'm going out. I'm determined to see Fort William when it isn't raining—even if it *is* three o'clock in the morning. Come on, Paddy Dolan!'

She dragged the reluctant but obliging Paddy out of bed, and together they dressed and went out into the summer night. As Paddy had said, it really had stopped raining, and the scent of honeysuckle was everywhere. Fort William lay as if under a spell, its empty streets bathed in moonlight. The loch was like a silver shield, its waters unruffled, and above the little town rose the great mountain, not of an especially graceful shape, it is true, but still of an undoubted majesty—especially when you couldn't see the disfiguring aluminium works upon its flank.

'Well, we can always say we've *seen* him,' declared Annette triumphantly. 'And if you can go by what you hear, that's quite a feat!'

## The Road to the Isles

I WOULD like to be able to tell you that it was fine when they left Fort William, but I'm afraid I can't. It was raining as usual. Not gentle rain either, but great heavy drops that fell, plop, into the loch and covered it with silver rings, like shillings. The top of the Ben was covered with the usual ominous black cloud; the trees dripped; the road squelched; the gutters gurgled. It was as if Fort William was determined to live up to its reputation as one of the wettest spots in Great Britain!

They trooped down to the little station and stood disconsolately beside their luggage. If it hadn't been for the baskets labelled THEATRICAL COSTUMES, nobody would have guessed that they were ballet-dancers. They looked more like a boarding-school going back after the holidays, and homesick at that! Even Madame Boccaccio, in the old-fashioned cape she always wore, might have been one of the mistresses—that is, until she moved. *Then* you knew her for what she was. No matter what strange garment Anya Boccaccio put upon her body (and she certainly did turn up in some queer costumes, her favourite being a long black skirt with a froth of off-white petticoats underneath that showed when she sat down, and funny little black-buttoned boots), whatever she wore, it didn't hide her grace.

The train arrived, and they all piled into the carriages. It was quite full, so they had to separate. Madame Boccaccio, as befitted her age and rank, travelling first-class in solitary splendour. The others climbed, by ones and twos, into the third-class carriages. Annette, Paddy, Hans and Charles found themselves together.

' "It's by Sheil water the track is to the west,
    By Ailort and by Morar to the sea, . . . " '

sang Paddy. 'Do you folks know that this is the Road to the Isles? Och, and it's often I've wished to take it!

77

' "Sure, by Tummel and Loch Rannoch and Lochaber I
   will go,
   By heather tracks wi' heaven in their wiles;
   If it's thinkin' in your inner heart braggart's in my
   step,
   You've never smelt the tangle o' the Isles." '

'What is tangle?' asked Annette. 'I've often wondered.'
'Sure, and it's the seaweed, and the "braggart" is the
swank that's in your bearing. Och, and it's glad I am to be
taking the Road to the Isles!'
'I'd take the road to anywhere, as long as it's out of Fort
William and this rain,' said Annette, settling in her corner
and holding up a copy of the *Dancing World* so that it hid
the wet view. 'Tell me, someone, when we get to Mallaig.'
A sunburnt young climber, with a couple of enormous
framed rucksacks wedged precariously into the rack above
his head, and two large feet clad in nailed boots, regarded
her pityingly. Evidently the poor child had no idea that
this journey from Fort William to Mallaig was one of the
most wonderful in the world. For a short while there was
silence in the compartment. The young climber studied
an Ordnance Survey map and made notes on the back of
an envelope; an old lady, dressed in a large plaid cap,
turned the heel of a sock; Annette and her companions
(Paddy, and the two male dancers Hans and Charles) read
their respective papers. No-one, except the climber, noticed
that the rain had stopped, and the sun had come out. The
train was winding through a deep gorge, in the bottom of
which glinted the silver thread of a stream, and beside it
a narrow white ribbon of a road. All around was an
amphitheatre of mountains, some standing out, rocky,
uncompromising, others with their heads hidden in the
clouds. The shriek of the engine, echoed back by the
mountain walls, made Annette look up from her book.
'Oh!' she said, with a gasp. 'Why—why, it's beautiful!'
'Didn't you expect it to be?' said the climber in
amusement.
Annette regarded him with a pair of solemn dark eyes.
'No—not after Fort William,' she said.
'I know you won't believe me, but Fort William can be
beautiful too if you visit it in the right season,' said the
young man. 'You should come in May and judge it then.'

But Annette wasn't listening. She had glanced across out of the opposite window, and behold, a fairytale loch was floating past. Pink water-lilies embroidered its banks, exquisite little islands lay upon its surface and were reflected in its limpid waters. Some of the islets had Scotch pine trees upon them—one to each island—of fantastic shapes. Seen against the rain-washed sky, they looked like hobgoblin trees out of a fairytale book illustrated by Rackham.

'Loch Eilt,' said her companion, and smiled as Annette nearly fell over him in her eagerness to reach the window. 'And now you'd better come back to this side. You're missing quite a lot over here.'

And so she was! Before her excited eyes appeared places of unbelievable beauty, all with the most fascinating names (the young climber explained them all). The Nose of the Wee Hill of the Sheiling was the name of the tiny clachan down by the winding road leading to Lochailort. The soaring mountains, silhouetted against the sky, were Roshven and the Stac, Druim Fiaclach and Sgurr na Ba Glas (the Peak of the Grey Cow), and here were the rocky shores of Loch Ailort itself. The next forty minutes were spent by Annette dashing from one side of the compartment to the other, in determination not to miss anything. Paddy and the two young male dancers followed her example rather more decorously.

Lochailort . . . Beasdale . . . Arisaig . . . the lovely little villages slid past, as the train slowly, slowly, drew its load of passengers round the edges of precipitous gorges and down to the Western sea. Now they were on a hollow-sounding bridge, with the ground falling away beneath them and the roar of a cataract in their ears (they had the windows wide open by this time). Now they were winding round the shoulder of a great mountain, the back end of the train curling slowly after them like an outsize in caterpillars. Now they were plunging through glorious woodlands, passing lonely, narrow, sea-lochs with rocky shores and glistening white sands. And here was the open sea itself and a strange blue island with a hooked top.

'That's the Sgurr of Eigg,' said the climber. 'Not spelt like the domestic egg! And farther over to the right there is Rhum. The mountains you can see are the Cuillin of Rhum. They're not as high as the Cuillin of Skye, but very fine all the same. As a matter of fact, that's where I'm going now. I'm travelling by way of Portree. I've always wanted to see the capital of Skye. It will mean that I shall have to cross the Cuillin to Glen Brittle, and get the Soay boatman to take me over to Rhum.'

'What? Cross the mountains with that huge pack?' gasped Annette.

'Oh, no! I shall send it round by Sligachan on Macrae's bus,' laughed her companion. 'By the way, this is Morar Bay. I expect you've heard of "The White Sands of Morar"?'

Of course she hadn't. Why had no-one told her that on the west coast were fairytale bays, and coves with sands as white as sugar?

'Why,' said Annette, 'I thought for the moment that it had been snowing!'

'When you run the sand through your fingers it glistens,' went on the young man, 'and you're left with the stuff glittering on your hands—like the "frost" you buy at Christmas-time to put on the Christmas tree. That's the mica in it. Well, we shall be at Mallaig in a few minutes. Look over there—can you see the island with the jagged mountains? That is Skye and the Black Cuillin.'

'I never thought it would be like this,' said Annette, as they drew into the little station. 'It's far more exciting and beautiful than anything I imagined.'

Oh, the charm of Mallaig! Fishy it might be, cold and rainy it might be on most days of the year, but today the sun had come out, and Mallaig was the most fascinating place in the world. So thought Annette, as she strode down towards the quay. Drawing alongside was a little white steamer with the name LOCH NEVIS upon its side, and sunburnt sailors making fast ropes and chains, and bearing the magic words MACBRAYNE upon their jerseys, while Gaelic oaths fell from their lips. (Well, if they weren't oaths, they sounded like it!)

'I'll tell you a funny verse about MacBrayne,' said Annette's companion as they waited for the gangway to be lowered. 'It's this:

' "The earth it is the Lord's, and all that it contains,
    Except the piers and ferry-boats, and they are all
        MacBrayne's".'

Mallaig was certainly noisy, Annette decided, but it was the most romantic noise imaginable. Seagulls, circling in an ever-changing cloud round the funnels of the steamer, screamed. Chains clanked; the gangway clattered as it came down and was secured to the quayside. A crowd of people came ashore, chattering in several different languages. And what exciting people! Climbers with enormous rucksacks, like her companion's own, with ice-axes sticking out of them, and coils of rope over their shoulders. Some of them wore funny little round caps of wool with pom-poms on the top, and all wore heavy nailed boots which clattered on the cobbles. Scotsmen in kilts, and Scotsmen in long tartan trousers (the trews, explained the young hiker). Scotswomen wearing tartan cloaks and strong brogue shoes. Sightseers in very new Scottish woollies (obviously bought on the trip). Businesslike people taking photographs, and vague-looking people (authors, maybe) writing down things in note-books. Yet more people sending off picture postcards. Added to these was a party of American tourists who dubbed everything, from Mallaig to Scotland itself, as 'cute'. There was also a bus trip, complete with bus.

And now came the most exciting part of all (in Annette's eyes, anyway)—the unloading of the cargo. You wouldn't believe the things that came out of that small steamer! It was indeed like the Noah's Ark. Crates of hens, a pig, a litter of puppies, and a mewing cat in a basket. Also it was evident that someone was moving house, and in a very short time most of their household belongings were standing on the cobbles of the little jetty. There was a baby's wooden cradle (how many little Highlanders had been rocked to sleep in that by some gentle Highland mother, singing a strange Gaelic lullaby?). There was an old bedstead, complete with feather mattress ('thank goodness for a fine day!' thought Annette), a steel fender glinting in the sunshine, a table with a hollow in the middle for the potatoes and another smaller hollow for the salt! You didn't bother with plates, and indeed, why should you, when you were eating off a table scrubbed to such snowy whiteness it positively made you blink? Annette's climber friend explained all these details—he had taken quite a fancy to the child. She was so unsophisticated, so thrilled with everything, and not ashamed to show it either. He

81

made up his mind, there and then, to postpone his visit to Rhum for a day and stay in Portree, so that he could see her dance (oh, yes, he had heard all about the Skye Gathering Ball, and the exciting fact that Annette was dancing the principal rôle of La Sylphide). Of course it would mean having to stay the whole of Sunday in the tiny capital—there is no travel on the Sabbath Day in Skye, as we have said before—but it was worth it. He wanted, above all things, to see her dance. . . .

'And now look—the new cargo is going to be hoisted aboard,' he said, as the last possession of the unknown mover was deposited carefully on the quayside to be collected later on. It happened to be a photograph of Prince Charles and Princess Anne. Yes, folk from Skye and the Outer Isles are loyal in the extreme. 'Someone's taking their car across. Now for some fun!'

First they swung the little crane over the edge of the quay, then four rings of chains were placed in position, and these were in turn covered with sacking to protect the car wheels. With many exhortations to the nervous driver —an American, to judge by the magnificence of his automobile—the car was sidled on to the extreme edge of the jetty, its wheels resting on the four sacks. Then, with a succession of Gaelic oaths (Annette insisted that they were oaths), the sailors, helped by several interested onlookers, hoisted the gleaming car aloft and over the side of the steamer on to the fore-deck, where it came to rest, looking like an exotic beetle.

'It takes up an awful lot of space, doesn't it?' said Annette anxiously. 'I only hope there's room for us as well!' She looked round her at the crowd of passengers who were now streaming up the gangway.

'You needn't worry,' laughed the young man. 'The *Loch Nevis* is bigger than she looks. There's room for quite a lot of passengers besides the cargo.'

In a short time they were steaming up the Sound of Sleat. On one side were the mighty mountains and winding sea-lochs of Knoydart and Kintail. The climber told Annette their fascinating names—this one was Loch Nevis, the Loch of Heaven, and the one they were coming to farther on was Loch Hourn, the Loch of Hell. The two great mountains—one on the north and one on the south of Loch Hourn—were Ben Sgriol and Ladhar-Bheinn. On the other side, over the blue sea, the Cuillin Hills of Skye ran across the horizon like the jagged edge of a saw. The flat peninsula of Sleat stood out so clearly that you could see every small house and croft upon it, each looking like a doll's house, or a little toy farm out of a Noah's Ark. The Sound narrowed, the mountains closed in upon the little steamer until you felt you could step over her side on to the mainland.

'This is Kylerhea, where there is a ferry,' said the young climber, who had followed Annette to the rail. 'At least there is usually a ferry, but I am told it's not functioning at the moment because they're making up the road over Glen Arroch. It's the old drovers' road, and it's a fearsome climb even for a modern car. The mountain is called Beinn na Caillich, the Hill of the Old Woman. Skye folk are fond of old women, it seems. There are two Beinn na Caillichs in the Isle. The other one is above Broadford, and they say a Norse princess was buried upon the top.'

Presently they came to Kyle of Lochalsh, where some of the passengers disembarked, and others came aboard. Above Kyleakin—the village on the Skye side of the strait —was the ruin of an ancient building.

'That's Castle Maol,' said the climber, who seemed to be a positive mine of information. 'Another of Skye's old women lived there. She was a Norse princess too, and she was known as Saucy Mary. It's said she used to close the Strait by stretching a great chain across it, and then demanding harbour dues from the ships that wanted to pass through. Quite an effective way of making money! The natives will show you the marks on the rocks where they say the chain was fastened.'

The steamer was off again, passing between the mainland of Skye, and the islands of Scalpay and Raasay lying off her eastern seaboard. It was nearly five o'clock when they got to Portree, the little capital of Skye. It proved to be a small village (though to the inhabitants of Skye it is a town), very prettily situated, with one or two hotels, a sleepy main street and a wide market-square with a busstand at one side. Outside the shops and in the bus-stand stood placards giving visitors to the island information about the various tours. For a few shillings you could go to Flodigarry and the Flora MacDonald country, and see the wonderful Kilt Rock and Duntulm Castle, the ancient

83

seat of the MacDonalds, once Lords of Skye and of the Isles. Or you could go to the weird Quairang and see on your way the Old Man of Storr, mighty pillar of stone, towering up one hundred and fifty feet at the foot of his Storr precipices. Or, going west, you could visit Dunvegan Castle, seat of MacLeod of MacLeod, whose flag, so the guide will tell you, was given to a former MacLeod chief by a fairy whom he married. 'Och, yes, and here is the Fairy Bridge where they said farewell to one another, for she went back to fairyland after a wee while.' Or you could go to Elgol and visit remote Loch Coruisk, whose dark waters are entirely enclosed by the precipices of the Black Cuillin. On the way you would pass the old island fortress of Airdrochan Castle, with its rocky causeway connecting it with the mainland. Oh, the wonders you could see in Skye for the matter of a few shillings!

But none of these wonders were for Annette and her companions. They were here to dance, not to see the beauties of this romantic island. They must first of all find a room to rehearse in. After this they would be free to go to their lodgings (these had already been found for them by the Skye Gathering Ball Committee) and rest for a short while before the work of the evening began. They had, of course, had a meal on board the steamer. The young climber set off to find a lodging for himself, having assured Annette that he would be at the ball tonight by hook or by crook. If no tickets were to be had, he would masquerade as a waiter!

# PART TWO

## 'La Sylphide'

WELL, here we are back again at the Skye Gathering Ball, but now we know why Annette happened to be in Skye at all, and why she was dancing the chief rôle in the ballet, *La Sylphide*, when another dancer's name was on the bills.

When the door leading to the dressing-rooms closed behind Annette in her shabby mackintosh, the scene changed. Instead of glamorous guests in ball-dresses and Highland costumes, here were the artistes getting ready for their performance. Girls making up their faces, necks and shoulders with grease-paint; doing their arms and shoulders with 'wet white'. Here were men 'drawing in' their eyes with eyebrow-pencils; girls pulling up tights; girls tying up point-shoes. Here were dancers (male and female) making use of chairs to 'warm up'. Annette was late. First, she had been waylaid by her friend, the climber, who hadn't been able to get a ticket after all. In any case he hadn't any evening clothes with him, and for that reason also the 'waiter' stunt wouldn't work either. Besides, take a look at his boots! Annette burst into a peal of laughter at the sight of them. They looked so out of place among all the dancing-pumps and ballet-shoes! Oh, well, the only thing left to do was to smuggle him into the men's dressing-room. After this, as we know, she had run into Sheena and the Slaughter party, and had had to stand and make polite conversation while the precious minutes fled by. She must hurry, hurry!

Off came her everyday clothes, to be flung down any-where—on the floor mostly, I'm ashamed to say. Annette wasn't at all particular about her ordinary clothes. But oh, the care she took pulling up her tights to creaseless per-fection, the tidiness of her shoe ribbons, the neatness of the roll of hair in the hair-net under the flowery wreath! Oh, the care she took to hold the ankle-length white dress, so that not a frill should be crushed (and woe betide anybody who came too near and brushed against her!).

And now came the all-important matter of her make-up. She had put on the 'foundation' before putting on her dress, but the finishing touches could not be added until the very last minute for fear they should become smudged. Annette was a master hand at make-up by now. She had profited by all the advice and criticisms of her friends. She knew exactly how much No. 4 to use for her eyes, and where to place No. 9, the rouge to accentuate her high cheek-bones.

'No false eyelashes,' she said aloud, staring at her reflection in the glass. 'The audience is too near. But I must have a lot of pale make-up, so as to give the illusion of a spirit. That's what was wrong with Simonetta—she was too *earthly*. . . . Oh, please God, make it a success tonight! It's my very last time, so please, *please* make them like me. . . .'

Well, Annette's prayer was answered. The Skye Gathering Ball audience was a quite different proposition from the Fort William one. For one thing, it was much more sophisticated. Almost all the Skye guests had been educated in England, or at some famous Scottish school or university. The other guests were, as Paddy had said, mostly Londoners (members of what is known as 'Society'). They were all extremely what Annette called 'ballet conscious'. which is perhaps why the committee had chosen to present a ballet in place of the usual cabaret. The audience loved Annette, from her entrance as the ethereal Spirit of the Scottish countryside to her exit as the sad little Sylphide, doomed to die. In fact, they loved the whole ballet, and they showed it. Thus encouraged, the little company gave of their best. The Scottish dancing by the *corps de ballet* was spirited as it had never been before, and no-one forgot to come in, perhaps because Annette was no longer in it, her place having been taken by Helen. Even James was likeable (and he is not, as a rule, a very sympathetic character). Gurn, as his perfidious Best-Man, who runs off with the Bride, was convincingly boorish. Yes, it all went better than it had ever gone before.

Paddy, as the Sugar Plum Fairy, received quite an ovation. Pandora, in her Black Swan *solo,* was clapped to the echo, which was some consolation to her, though she had never really forgiven Annette for gate-crashing into the *prima ballerina* rôle in the chief ballet, which ought, by rights, to have gone to her. Even Phillip Summerfield (a pale neat young man with a receding chin) came into his own in his *solo* from Swan Lake, and leapt as he had never leapt before! ('It's a fact,' thought Annette, watching him, 'there's always *something* a person can do, however unpromising they are, and it's a fact, Phillip can leap.') 'You'd hardly recognise him,' she said to Paddy as they waited behind the screens that hid them from the main part of the ballroom. 'Darling Phillip!'

'Or you, either, Annette,' said Paddy admiringly. 'Sure, an' it's a different creature you are, Annette Dancy, from the sad and spiritless Sylph you were at Fort William!'

'I think we all feel the change,' said Annette. 'An appreciative audience makes all the difference.'

After the ballet was over, and they had changed and removed their make-up, they were all invited to mingle with the dancers, and, of course, to partake of the buffet supper spread out in the supper-room.

'I'm all for that!' said Annette to Bill (she had found out her friendly climber's name by now). 'One *pirouette,* one sausage roll, is my rule! There's only one thing that worries me, Bill, and that's *you.* What are you going to do about your supper? It's really very awkward your not having a ticket, you know, because you can hardly eat their supper, can you, when you haven't paid anything? You see, I'm a clergyman's daughter, and it wouldn't be honest.'

Bill couldn't help laughing at Annette standing there, so ethereal in her white Sylphide dress (she hadn't yet changed), discussing of all things—sausage rolls and honesty!

'I've got an idea,' he said. 'I'll pinch a couple of sausage rolls, and a sandwich, and a cup of coffee, and you can give the management five bob from an anonymous donor. Here it is. . . .' He solemnly handed her two half-crowns.

'Oh, *thank* you, Bill, said Annette. 'That will solve everything.'

After they had finished supper and she had changed, they walked out into the soft warm Skye night. Annette said she felt like some fresh air. 'And in any case,' she added, 'I don't think I would "mingle" very well—not in this frock. I couldn't go in there and talk to Sheena and her smart friends in an old cotton frock, now could I?'

Bill, glancing down at the offending garment, said that it looked all right to him (and he meant it), but that he agreed with her first point—it was much nicer out here watching the lights glimmer in the harbour.

'There's a lovely white yacht riding at anchor down there,' said Annette. 'I've heard it belongs to Somebody Frightfully Important.' Unconsciously she was reverting to her way of speaking at her provincial dancing-school— how many times had she and her fellow students thrilled to the rumour of Somebody Frightfully Important in the studio? 'They say he's a film star, or something. At least the yacht doesn't actually belong to *him*, but he's one of the people on it.'

'Lucky man!' said Bill. 'What could be grander than sailing in these waters—unless it's climbing these mountains?' His eyes were on the dark shadow where the Cuillin blacked out the stars.

'You love climbing?' said Annette. 'Angus does too.'

'Angus?' repeated the young man. 'A friend of yours?'

'Oh, yes—a very great friend,' said Annette.

'You're not engaged to him, are you?'

Annette burst into a peal of laughter.

'Goodness, no! I'm not old enough to be engaged.'

'I thought you weren't,' said Bill, 'but when you were dancing you looked much older. You don't mind my asking, do you?'

'Oh no—of course not,' answered Annette. 'Why ever should I?'

The young man didn't answer, and suddenly Annette became aware of a strange silence between them, and she knew that in another minute Bill was going to behave just as Angus had done that night on the peel-tower roof, and that this time she, Annette, would be to blame.

'I must go,' she said quickly. 'Goodbye, dear Bill. It's been lovely meeting you. I do hope you have a nice time climbing on Rhum, and I'll remember to give your half-crowns to whoever it is on the committee.'

Bill looked after her regretfully. He forgot that he had thought her 'a funny plain little thing' when he had first seen her, and only knew that she was the first girl he had ever wanted to kiss. Yes, she was charming. It wasn't only her grace, and the fact that she was a dancer, but something else too—something that is quite indefinable, and that has nothing whatever to do with beauty, or riches, or age, but which makes a person beloved wherever they go, or however old they are.

Someone else thought Annette charming too—a middle-aged man in evening dress, with hair going grey at the temples, and a small military moustache. After the supper interval he asked one of the members of the committee the name of the principal dancer in the ballet, *La Sylphide*.

'I'm sorry but I can't tell you her name, sir,' answered the Scotsman, who happened to be in a hurry. Then he remembered that this man was one of the party in the yacht anchored in the harbour, and that he had already received a generous cheque from the owner towards the Sky Gathering funds, and tried his best to be helpful. 'I expect I can find out for you.' He took the guest's arm and led him out into the lobby, and over to the fireplace, beside which a notice of the ball was pinned. 'Here you are, sir,' he said, pointing out the name of the *ballerina* placed at the top of the list of dancers. '*Guest Artist, Mlle Simonetta Delgarno—La Sylphide. . . . Producer, Georges Reinholt Dutoit. Assistant Producer and ballet-mistress, Mme Anya Boccaccio. . . .* These dancers are just students, you know, sir, but I think myself they're first-rate. Yes, I'm glad you think so too. They're from the school run in conjunction with the Cosmopolitan Ballet—all of them, that is, except Mademoiselle Delgarno. She was with the De Cuevas Ballet, I believe.' The Scotsman felt quite proud of knowing so much, though he *had* read it up only that afternoon on the back of the programme. 'The school is in the same building as the theatre, if that is any help to you, sir. That's in Beaufort Street, of Oxford Circus.'

The stranger was busily writing down these details—on his shirt cuff, of all places! (A very dirty habit, thought the young Highlander disapprovingly. He had been carefully brought up by strict Scottish parents.) Having finished his writing, the older man murmured his thanks and turned to go.

'Oh, you're not leaving us yet, I hope?' said the Scotsman. 'It's only eleven o'clock.'

'I'm afraid so,' said the other. 'We're weighing anchor at dawn, you see, so we're turning in early.'

'*Bon voyage!*' said the Scot. 'And many thanks for coming, sir.'

'Goodbye,' the stranger said, and left the building, nearly colliding with a girl coming in the opposite direction. She looked up at him, startled.

'Oh, I am so sorry,' he said.

'So am I!' laughed Annette. 'I expect I was going too fast, as usual.'

The stranger saw the touches of make-up still round her dark eyes. Then she was one of the dancers in the ballet? For a second he thought of asking her where he could find Mlle Delgarno, but she had already gone, threading her way gracefully between the guests, who were coming out to have a breath of fresh air.

'Oh, well,' thought the stranger, 'it doesn't really matter. I've got all the information I want here.' He looked down at his cuff and smiled as he made his way down to the harbour.

## The Invitation

ALL the members of the Slaughter party enjoyed the ball except Sheena. To be sure, she had danced every dance, and had received enough compliments to turn the head of any girl less used to them than herself. But the sad fact remained—Jamie hadn't asked her for a single dance. He'd danced with Deborah—yes, five times, thought Sheena, counting jealously, and he'd danced with Elspeth and Flora, and even with Catriona who squinted, and Mairi who couldn't keep time with the music. It was humiliating! And then at the very end of the ball an even worse thing had happened. That plain little Annette

Dancy, whom she'd tried for very shame to keep out of the sight of their party, had come up and talked, and had made friends with Deborah and her mother.

'Oh, we just loved your dancing, Annette—we *may* call you Annette, mayn't we? We thought it was just marvellous. The Scottish bits were ever so good too. Jaimie said so, didn't you, Jaimie? He's an expert on Highland dancing, you know. . . . Oh, haven't you two met? I was taking it for granted you had. This is Jaimie Gordon, Annette.'

Jaimie Gordon? It sounded familiar, but Annette couldn't think where she'd heard the name before.

'How do you do?' she said in her old-fashioned way, and held out her hand. 'I'm so glad you liked the ballet.'

And then Jaimie had asked her to dance—yes, Annette, in her shabby cotton frock, while she, Sheena Macdonald, in her glittering white ball-dress, looked on. But there was worse to come. When the dance ended, Jaimie brought his partner back to Mrs. Slaughter's side and bowed with old-world courtesy.

'You do indeed dance beautifully,' he said to Annette. 'If you had been staying on the island until Friday I could have taken you to the *ceilidh* at Ardavasar, where you would have seen some good Highland dancing.' (Oh, the jealousy that burned in Sheena's heart! Annette to be taken to the *ceilidh* by the famous Cock o' the North. Unthinkable! Fortunately it couldn't happen.)

'Annette is going home to England the day after tomorrow,' she put in quickly.

'Yes, it would have been tomorrow,' laughed Annette, 'but you know what it is in Scotland, and in the Highlands in particular—you simply can't *move* on the Sabbath!'

'Don't we know it!' exclaimed Mamie Slaughter. 'Well, it sure is a pity. We'd have liked fine if you could have come and stayed with us. Deborah's taken such a fancy to you, and any friends of Debbie's are sure friends of ours.'

'Yes, you could have stayed at our castle,' put in Deborah. 'Of course, it's Jaimie's castle really,' she added, much to Sheena's disgust. (Now why need the stupid girl have told Annette that? She'd be more keen on the young man than ever.) 'We've rented it for the season, and it sure is old and *romantic*' (she put the accent on the first

91

syllable). 'I jest know you'd adore Airdrochan Castle, Annette.'

'Airdrochan Castle?' repeated Annette. 'Gordon of Airdrochnish . . .'

'That is myself,' said Jaimie, with a little bow and a query in his voice.

'Oh, but it can't be!'

'Why can it not be?' pursued the young man.

'You *can't* be the friend Angus was talking about,' said Annette. 'That would be too queer. And yet of course it wouldn't be queer really. This is Skye, and it was Skye Angus was talking about.'

'Are you speaking of Angus MacCrimmon?' said Jaimie. 'If so, he is my friend, and he has come yesterday to stay with me. I have tried to persuade him to come to the ball, but he would not.'

'If he'd known I was dancing he'd have come,' said Annette. She wasn't being conceited, she was just stating facts.

'I expect he would,' said Jaimie with a smile. 'Angus is often speaking about you to me.'

All this Sheena heard, and was consumed with hatred for Annette. First Angus, then Jaimie. How many more young men did the girl want? Fortunately Sheena did not know about Bill, the climber.

'Well, it seems to me more than ever a pity that you can't stay with us,' said Mamie Slaughter. 'Jaimie, can't you persuade her.'

But now Annette didn't need any persuading. The fact of Angus being there changed everything. The Slaughters and Jaimie Gordon were suddenly like old friends.

'If you really mean it,' she said, 'I can stay with you for a whole week. You see . . .' Then she told them all about what Marie called the 'fall-through of Dundee', and the resulting extra week's holiday. 'And Mummy won't be expecting me for another week at least,' she added.

'Then that's settled,' said Mamie Slaughter, pleased that her darling Deborah should have got what she wanted, and indeed she was very pleased herself to have the dear child to stay with them. It would liven things up. There were many empty spare bedrooms at Airdrochan Castle, and Mamie (like most Americans) was a friendly soul. She liked them all full of guests. The trouble was that people just didn't drop in for the week-end at Airdrochan —it was far too remote.

'Wa-al, then we can get goin',' she said, as the band played Auld Lang Syne. 'We'll have to find Pop. He'll be somewhere about.'

Eventually Pop was tracked down, fast asleep in the sitting-out room. Jaimie, who had gone in search of him, marvelled at the docility of American husbands where their wives and pretty daughters were concerned. Here was Abraham Slaughter, the maker of a million dollars and more, meekly accompanying his family to a Highland ball (of all things), just because they'd drawled in their lazy language, 'Oh, Pop—it sure will look mighty queer if you don't show up.' Yes, thought Jaimie, in their own words it was 'mighty queer'. The girl *he* married would go where *he* wanted. He would be master in his own house. His dark eyes rested on Sheena, and they grew soft. She'd looked a perfect picture at the ball tonight in her glittering white dress. He'd wanted to dance every dance with her, but he had sworn he would teach her a lesson, and, when his mind was made up, he didn't change it. But no matter! At the *ceilidh* at Ardavasar he would rectify matters.

So it happened that instead of returning to her lodging Annette was packed into the front seat of the Slaughters' big car, between Deborah and Murdo (who acted as the Slaughters' chauffeur, Pop not having any great liking for the Skye roads, especially at night). Soon they were speeding along the desolate moorland roads, and round the seemingly endless lochs towards Airdrochnish. As they went, Deborah pointed out to Annette all the local landmarks, much to Murdo's silent amusement at her pronunciation.

'That's the Sligachan Hotel,' she said, as the headlamps picked out a lonely building standing beside a bridge under a great round mountain. 'We had dinner there this evening before coming on to the ball. The mountain's name is Glamaig. You can't see it properly just now, but in daylight you'd think the folks had poured a lot of custard sauce over it!' (Indignant snort from the outraged Murdo.) 'And way up there'—she pointed over to the right—'is Glen Sligachan, where there was an awful show-down between the clans. The MacDonalds and the MacLeods, it was. They're the chief clans in the island, you know. Well,

93

the MacDonalds won, and, as we say back home, the MacLeods sure had it! I think it's jest cute, don't you, the way folk over here remember all the things that happened hundreds and hundreds of years ago. D'you know, there's a boulder way up that glen called the Bloody Stone, and the stream is called the Allt Dearg, or Red Burn, because of all the blood! Can you beat that?'

'We are pronouncing it Allt Jerrack,' said Murdo solemnly, unable any longer to hear his native tongue so mispronounced.

Round and round the lochs went the car, now down beside the seaweedy shore, where the moonlight glittered on the waves, now crawling dizzily along the ledge-like road, a hundred feet or more above the water.

'This is Broadford,' said Deborah, as the headlamps picked out a small collection of houses and a hotel. 'It's our nearest big village. Gosh, I wish you could see it in daylight! It's too cute for anything. The people here call it a "town". Waal, we wouldn't call it that back home, but it sure is awful pretty. We turn off here, and in a minute we come to a lochan with water-lilies on it—yes, here it is. It's called Loch Cill Chriosd (the Loch of Christ) which is funny because it's supposed, like most of Skye's lochs, to be haunted by a dreadful water-horse that comes up behind you, and then drags you down to his watery lair underneath the loch. That's right, isn't it, Murdo?'

'That iss so,' agreed the soft-voiced Murdo. 'No-one will walk beside the loch after nightfall.'

'Yes, and they really believe it,' went on Deborah. 'The folk who live here, I mean. You do yourself, don't you, Murdo?'

'Naturally I am believing it,' said Murdo. 'Many people there are who are seeing the *each dubh*, and those who are seeing him are not long for this world. Yes indeed it is so, and I can tell you I am not at all wishful to see him for myself.' He put his foot on the accelerator, and the car shot forward, leaving the lonely lochan behind in a very short time. Deborah turned to Annette and gave her a broad wink that could be seen in the bright moonlight.

'There! What did I tell you?'

'You would be doing better to point out to the lassie the grand mountain on the right,' said Murdo reproachfully.

He knew quite well that Deborah was laughing at him. 'Oh, yes, look over there, Annette—its name is Blaven.' From the back of the car came Sheena's low voice:

> ' "Oh, Blaven, rocky Blaven,
> How I long to be with you again,
> To see lashed gulf and gully
> Smoke white in the windy rain." '

Even her jealousy and the soreness of her heart could not prevent her from singing her beloved mountain's praises. 'That poem was written by Alexander Smith, and I shall sing it at the *ceilidh*.'

Annette said nothing. She was lost in wonder at the great mountain rising up before them. Ben Nevis? Why, he was like a pillow compared with this rugged giant! The moonlight made him seem even more awe-inspiring, as it picked out the deep gulfs and gashes seaming his northern flanks.

'We're nearly home,' said Deborah. 'There's the castle. See it? Over there by the loch. We'll be at the bottom of the causeway in a minute. Someone will have to get out and open the gate.'

'Surely Murdo can do it?' said Sheena. She would never have dreamed of opening a gate if one of her clansmen was there to do it for her, even if it meant that he had to get out of the car on purpose. Neither, let it be said, would Murdo have expected her to do so. But with Deborah it was different. He was no kin to the Slaughters. but was merely paid a wage (though a magnificent one, it is true) for driving their car. If they asked him to open the gate, he opened it, but he didn't do it without being told. There was a subtle difference, though it is doubtful whether Murdo could have explained it, and certainly the Slaughters wouldn't have understood him if he had. They were far too simple and straightforward to appreciate the intricacies of Highland kinship.

D ESPITE the hectic time she had had the day before, Annette was up early next morning. For one thing, there was so much to see, and for another she wanted to meet Angus. Besides, she was really in Skye, and this was exciting in itself. Even her bedroom was an adventure! It boasted an enormous four-poster bed, with a wooden box at the foot where (so Deborah had told her the night before) the former Gordon chieftains kept their claymores. These, Deborah had explained, were the great swords with which they cleft their enemies in twain, and they were never parted from them even in sleep—thus the box at the bed-foot! There were tapestry curtains to the bed, worked by Ishbel Gordon while her lord was away fighting at the Crusades. 'They were supposed to be fighting a Holy War,' Deborah had said the night before, when she had shown Annette her room, 'but it's my opinion they jest liked the fighting!' The bed itself consisted of a huge feather mattress, out of which Annette rose like Venus from the foam. The room had two windows in deep embrasures, and they were fitted with double frames to keep out the cold winter winds. They looked out over Loch Slapin, and beyond that to Blaven, whose rocky head could just be seen sticking out of a bank of rosy cloud. On his right the jagged spires of Clach Glas soared into the clear air like some Gothic cathedral. Directly below, the wavelets of the sea-loch lapped against the rugged walls of the castle, and a couple of seagulls rocked gently to and fro on the tide, fast asleep. It was a peaceful scene, rather as if even the Cuillin of Skye knew that it was the staircarpet on the shallow treads. On the bottom flight, leading into the square hall, the Slaughters had laid down a wide soft carpeting of a very modern design, which looked most out of place but which certainly 'kept the cold out of your feet', as Mamie Slaughter put it. Once Sabbath Day, thought Annette as she dressed.

'I must find Angus,' she said as she closed her bedroom door softly, and crept down the great stone staircase with its family portraits on the walls, and its traces of crimson out of the massive front door, she set off down the causeway to the road. Before leaving the ball last night she had asked Jaimie Gordon exactly where he lived while his castle was occupied, and his directions were clear in her mind. At the bottom of the causeway you turned to the left through the village, and up the rough track to the top of the hill behind. Then, when you got there, you would see the cottage below you, nestling cosily in a hollow of the hillside opposite. She had asked Jaimie not to tell Angus she was here—she wanted to surprise him. She certainly did so! Even the reserved Angus couldn't conceal his amazement and delight when she appeared at the cottage door—just as if it was quite an ordinary thing that she, Annette Dancy, should be in Skye, and at his very door at seven o'clock on a Sabbath morning!

'*Mo caileag dubh!*' he exclaimed. Then added, '*Mo chridhe.*'

'Oh, that sounds lovely!' exclaimed Annette. 'Say it again, Angus, please.'

Angus did so obligingly.

'And now translate it for me, please.'

'*Mo caileag dubh* means my little black-haired girl,' said Angus, but he didn't translate the other words, merely drawing Annette into the tiny living-room and pulling out a chair for her.

'And now tell me how it is that you are here,' he said. 'I suppose by some queer chance you have met the Slaughters?'

'Yes, that's it,' answered Annette. 'I think they're such kind people, and I think Deborah's sweet.' Then she told him all about the tour and how it had ended up at Portree instead of Dundee. 'And that's how I'm here,' she finished. 'The Slaughters were at the ball, and when they heard I had a week's extra holiday they invited me to stay at their castle—I mean Jaimie's castle—for as long as I liked. So I can go climbing with you, Angus—that is, if you'll take me.'

'But of course I shall take you climbing,' said Angus. 'You shall climb right up to the top of Blaven tomorrow, if you wish, and Jaimie will come too. It is his free day.'

'Oh . . .' Annette looked a little nervous. 'Blaven? Don't you think Blaven is—is rather a big mountain for me to

97

start on? Wouldn't the little one, the one at the end with the points on—be better?'

'Och, you are meaning Clach Glas?' laughed Angus. 'No, no, *mo chridhe,* I am not taking any little black-haired girl up yon dangerous peak. Clach Glas is for mountaineers only.'

'What does *mo chridhe* mean?' demanded Annette. 'You are always saying it.'

'It means—well, never mind what it means just now,' said Angus, coaxing the peat fire into a blaze. 'Some day, perhaps, I shall be telling you. Do you take sugar in your tea?'

'No, thank you,' said Annette. 'It's too fattening. I have to think very seriously about my figure these days, you know.'

'Figure? I shouldn't have thought you had one!' laughed Angus. 'Not what people round here call a "figure" anyway. You should be seeing Janet MacLeod. She is like a walking feather-bed. Jaimie says he is always expecting her to take flight and go sailing away over the mountains!'

'That reminds me,' put in Annette, 'where is Jaimie? This *is* his home, isn't it? You did say you were staying with him?'

'Castle Airdrochan is Jaimie's home,' corrected Angus. 'But yes, you are right—this is his cottage, and it is where he lives while the Slaughters are in the castle. But he is already gone out. Jaimie works very hard, you know, and just now, while I am here, he is wishful to have a little free time to spend with me, so he is beginning his day early.'

'Even the Sabbath Day?' laughed Annette. 'I thought no-one did any work on the Sabbath Day in Skye. Mamie Slaughter says they don't.'

'Not ordinary work,' agreed Angus, 'but the work of a veterinary surgeon does not stop even on the Sabbath Day —the calving of Douglas MacKinnon's cow, for instance. It is fortunate that it is growing light at about four o'clock in the morning just now. We are both getting up and are doing the housework, so as to have it all done before breakfast-time.'

'Yes, everything does look frightfully neat and clean,' said Annette, looking round 'Do you do it all yourselves?'

'Och, yes,' answered Angus. 'We are both very good

about the house—*bean-an-tighe*, as they say in the Gaelic. We can wash up, and make the beds, trim the lamps, yes, and make the porridge too. Will you stay and have breakfast with us, Annette? Jaimie should be back any moment now.'

'The Slaughters don't have breakfast until nine o'clock on Sundays,' said Annette, 'and then they have it in bed. Mamie says the Scottish Sabbath is very long and depressing for her, so she stays in bed for as much of it as she can! I think it's rather nice myself. It's so peaceful. . . . Oh, yes, I'd love to have breakfast with you, Angus; I can always have another one with the Slaughters later on.'

'What about the "figure"?' teased Angus.

When Jaimie came in about five minutes later he found Angus and Annette cooking the breakfast. Annette was making the toast and frying the bacon on the fire, while Angus stirred the porridge on the little oil-stove. He wouldn't trust Annette with this important task.

'Only Scotsmen know how to make porridge properly,' he declared. 'The Sassenachs are forgetting to put in the salt!'

'We make very good porridge on the Border,' Annette told him indignantly. 'We eat it with brown sugar and cream.'

'That is all wrong,' put in Jaimie solemnly (porridge is treated very seriously in the Highlands). 'Salt it should be, to bring out the flavour.'

They settled the argument by Angus and Jaimie having their porridge neat, as you might say, and Annette adding sugar.

Later on in the morning—a good deal later—Annette had a second breakfast in Mamie Slaughter's bedroom. She hadn't been there before and she gazed around her in amazement. The three long windows, in their deep stone embrasures, were hung with tartans of a glowing red and green. The curtains of the four-poster bed were in the same tartan. So far, so good. After this feast of Clan MacDonald, however, you came to the bed itself which was unadulterated Mamie Slaughter. On it was piled a huge puffy eiderdown of a pinky mauve satin, and the blankets, sheets and pillow-cases were all pale mauve to match. The

*Annette was frying bacon on the fire*

sheets were bound with the MacDonald tartan. The floor was covered right up to the walls with an Indian carpet of pale cream colour with raised pink flowers upon it, and the wallpaper (the Slaughters had had the room newly decorated for their stay) was a stripy satin, with appliques of floral subjects ornamenting the corners—the idea was that you felt you were in a conservatory. Round the room at varying intervals—growing shorter as they neared the bed—were a succession of oil-stoves: Mamie believed in being warm in her bedroom. When you opened the door, the scent of the room—warm paraffin-oil, ancient stone and Mamie's expensive French perfume—met you in a cloud.

'Come in, folks!' she cried warmly, heaving herself up in bed in a flurry of marabout-trimmed satin dressing-jacket. Incidentally the latter looked odd, to say the least, when you caught sight of her nightie in tartan silk underneath! 'Make yourself at home, do. Sit here, Annette.' She patted the billowing eiderdown invitingly. 'It sure is the warmest spot. My! My! Take a look at this breakfast —cold boiled ham! It's well to be seen it's the Scottish Sabbath. Even the domestics go on strike on the Sabbath Day! It's a wonder they don't jib at boiling the water for the coffee and serve you with a cold soft drink instead! Help yourselves, folks.'

Deborah, Sheena and Annette did as they were told, Annette managing to tuck away a very creditable slice of cold boiled ham and several slices of bread and butter, in spite of her earlier meal with Jaimie and Angus.

When she had recovered from the shock of the room, Annette began to take stock of the people in it. Apart from Mamie Slaughter, there was Sheena, her red-gold hair glinting in the morning sunlight, and Deborah, wearing a wonderful dressing-gown of écru lace with rosebud trimming and slippers trimmed with swansdown, and last (one might truly say least, as well) was Pop—a small grey silent figure, pathetic if only in contrast to the flowery opulence of his wife and daughter.

('Poor Pop!' thought Annette with a surge of pity for him. 'I wonder what he thinks about while he sits there at the window looking out at the mountains?')

Meanwhile Deborah and her mother were talking a hundred to the dozen. Mostly it was about the ball the

101

night before, and after they had exhausted that exciting topic it was about what they were going to do while Annette was staying with them.

'A whole week,' said Annette dreamily. 'In fact, a week and two days. I needn't go home till the Tuesday. At least——'

'At least what?' demanded Deborah.

'At least I expect it'll be all right for me to stay,' went on Annette, 'but of course when you're a dancer, you never know. A telegram may come for you any minute to say you're wanted for something.'

'What on earth could *you* be wanted for?' put in Sheena. 'I thought you were still only in the ballet-school?'

'Yes, so I am,' agreed Annette, 'but you see any time now they begin to hold the pantomime auditions, and there's some talk of a very special ballet programme on Children's Television, and they *say* the producer is going to call on our school for the children to illustrate it. I live in the hope of being chosen because I'm so small. But if it did happen, Paddy—she's my best friend—said she would be sure to send me a telegram so that I could dash back. I hope it doesn't happen while I'm here though, because it would be an awful long way to dash.'

'Yes, it would,' agreed Sheena, her green eyes resting on Annette's rather crumpled tweed skirt and much-washed jumper. What was there, she wondered, about this girl that made people notice her? Why, this morning she looked as plain as a pikestaff, yet all the time Deborah and her mother were planning expeditions to please her. She might be royalty, the amount of trouble they were taking! Then there was last night. . . . Sheena couldn't forget last night and the way Annette had stolen the picture.

'Tomorrow,' Deborah was saying, 'we could take the car to Elgol, hire a motor boat and take a look at Loch Coruisk. We've never been there, and they say it's swell.'

'It sounds lovely,' answered Annette, 'but do you think you could go on Tuesday instead? You see, it's Jaimie's free day, and he and Angus have promised to take me climbing tomorrow, and of course all of you too, if you would like to go.'

Sheena's green eyes regarded Annette jealously. There she was again! She hadn't been in the place more than five minutes before Angus was offering to take her climbing. And Jaimie, too. And fancy her knowing which was Jaimie's free day—she must have been up early and gone out to see them on the sly. The deceit of it!

'I hope you made it clear to them that you are a complete novice,' she said.

Annette stared back at her. Sheena was being even more unfriendly than usual.

'How do you know I *am* a novice?' she demanded. 'As a matter of fact I've climbed lots of hills in the Cheviots. One hill is just the same as another, even if it's in a different place.'

'That may be true of ordinary hills,' said Sheena, 'but it is not true of the Cuillin. They may be called "hills" but they are mountains really, and there is no easy way up any of them.'

'I suppose *you've* climbed them all?' retorted Annette. It was queer how Sheena always managed to rub her up the wrong way.

'Yes—most of them,' answered Sheena off-handedly. Then, as if the conversation had lost interest for her, she joined the silent head of the Slaughter family at the window, standing there and staring out at the lovely prospect of mountain and loch.

'I know what,' drawled Deborah. 'Let's *all* go climbing. I've never climbed a single thing, unless it's into the car, so we'll be novices together, Annette. If there are two of us they just can't go too fast.'

'I wish you girls would keep to the point,' grumbled Mamie from her downy pillows. 'I was just getting real stuck into this old i-tinary. Climbing tomorrow then, and over to Loch Whatsitsname the day after. Dunvegan Castle on Wednesday. On Friday there's the *ceilidh*. That leaves Thursday. We could go over to Duntulm and take a look at that. It says in the guide book that Flora MacDonald lived there, and folks back home are sure to want to know if we saw the place where *she* lived and the place where Bonnie Prince Charlie landed.'

Sheena, listening, marvelled at the way they got their facts all wrong. Duntulm was a MacDonald stronghold, it is true, but Flora never lived there. However she didn't correct them—she didn't consider them worth the bother.

The Slaughters talked on and on, making plans until every day had been filled up. They liked to feel that they were really 'showing' Skye to Annette, and they were far too simple and good-natured to realise that Sheena was despising them in her heart. What could the Slaughters see of the real Skye, thought the Scottish girl? What could they learn of this dark strange island by merely cruising round its winding haunted lochs, and along its stony roads in their gleaming 'convertible'? To be sure, they would go home and chatter about this and that, dubbing everything 'cute'—yes, from the Old Man of Storr to hoary Dunvegan Castle and its tattered Fairy Flag—and really imagine they had seen Skye. Oh, the happy Americans to be so easily pleased, thought Sheena, with a twist of her lips.

## Climbing Blaven

THEY all met after breakfast in the gun-room of the castle. Here they found quite an array of heavy boots, mackintoshes, rucksacks, and the like. It was easy to be seen that Jaimie and Angus had been busy!

'Say, folks, you don't mean I've got to wear these?' said Deborah, picking up a pair of nailed boots and wrinkling up her nose at them.

'Yes, indeed I do,' said Angus. 'You are not taking any liberties with the Cuillin Hills of Skye. It is bad enough to climb grassy mountains without the proper footwear, but here it is asking for trouble, as you will soon see when you have climbed one of these black peaks.'

Jaimie stood silently watching them, secretly amused, no doubt, at the picture they made trying on garments as if they were playing Charades or some such game. He and Angus were wearing kilts and wind-jackets, and each carried an enormous rucksack, into which were packed extra woollies for the whole party, besides food, and all the other impedimenta of the climber.

In half an hour they were ready to go, and a queer sight they were! Annette looked all feet. She hadn't been able to find a pair of boots small enough for her, so she had filled them up with socks. She wore a pair of Angus's shorts which she had pleated round her slender waist with a belt, since they were about twice too large for her. Above these she wore an ancient woolly jumper, and on her head a woolly cap of washed-out salmon colour. Deborah wore a pair of her mother's slacks, in which she looked like 'a rose in trousers', as Angus put it. Sheena stood apart, regarding them all scornfully. Although she was dressed for climbing, she still managed to look glamorous. She was wearing a pair of long dark ski-trousers, tucked into the tops of her neat black boots. Above these was a dull green waterproofed silk wind-jacket, with knitted welt and wrist-bands. She wore nothing on her head, but carried, dangling by its strings, a knitted cap with ear-pieces to fasten under the chin. In her rucksack, which lay open on the table, was a waterproof cape, lined with the MacDonald tartan (red and green). She wore gloves with knitted backs and thick suède palms, and the undersides of the fingers were of suède too. Annette was to find out the reason for this later on.

When they were dressed they left the room, Sheena and Jaimie in front and Angus behind, with Annette and Deborah walking stiffly in their unaccustomed footwear. Mamie Slaughter was at the main door of the castle to see them off, and Pop came and stood behind her, silent as usual. They crossed the old weed-grown courtyard and followed a twisting pathway down to the lochside, where there was a tiny jetty with a boat moored (Jaimie's boat that Sheena had seen out on the loch yesterday). It didn't take them long to row across the loch at this point, and very soon they were clambering out on the shingle and up on to the road.

'This has saved us a couple of miles' walk round the head of the loch,' explained Jaimie. 'We will now make straight for Coire Uaigneich, which is one of the routes up Blaven most suitable for the ladies.'

'Does that include me?' demanded Sheena indignantly. 'I have climbed nearly as many of the Cuillin peaks as you have, Jaimie Gordon. The only peak I have not climbed, at one time or another, is yon small wicked one.'

'Clach Glas?' said Jaimie, following her gaze. 'We shall see how you manage, and perhaps, if you are indeed as proficient as you say, I might take you down the northern face of Blaven to the col, and over the Pinnacle Ridge, while the others rest.'

Sheena began to enjoy herself. Although she considered this climb quite beneath her, yet she was able to show her prowess by lightly swinging up difficult stretches, while the others went round an easy way.

They stopped for a breather when they reached the upper corrie and looked back. Loch Slapin lay shimmering in the sunshine, and so calm and clear was it that each rock upon its banks looked at itself in the water, and there were two Castles Airdrochan, one of them upside down! On the causeway a small figure could be seen.

'Yonder is old Seumas MacDonald,' said Jaimie. 'He is my foster-brother and bears the same Christian name as myself. Seumas is the Gaelic for James, you know. He is part postman, and part shepherd. He takes round the letters in the morning, then rides his bicycle up the rough track to his sheiling on the southern slopes of Beinn na Caillich. He drives his sheep up on to the hill and brings them down at night, then rides his bicycle home again. ready for next morning. A very busy man is Seumas—for a Highlander! There are not many bicycles in Skye, you know,' he added, turning to Annette. 'The roads are too bad. Seumas's is the only one in Airdrochnish, and proud he is of it.'

'Yes, I expect you prefer horses,' laughed Annette.

'No, we are not riding much either,' he answered. 'We are much preferring our own feet—except, of course, your friend Angus here, who has taken to the riding. Well, we had better be moving on, if we want to reach the top of Blaven today.'

Soon they penetrated deep into the corrie, and a desolate place it was. Black fingers of scree reached down into its gloomy depths, and smooth glaciated boulders filled it up to the mouth. On the north side a great jagged pinnacle, jutting out from a glistening wall of rock, soared into the air.

'That is the Unclimbed Pinnacle,' explained Jaimie to the others. He did not add that its name was no longer a true one, since he had, as we know, climbed it only a few days ago. Sheena glanced across at him, but his dark eyes were unreadable. 'There is a golden eagle's nest there,' he went on. 'If we are lucky we may see the birds.' But they were not lucky, and the silence of the corrie remained unbroken by the rush of mighty wings.

'Oh, what queer rough rock!' cried Annette, as they clambered over a succession of enormous boulders. 'It's rough, like a nutmeg-grater!'

'It is called gabbro,' exclaimed Angus, 'It is this rock that makes climbing in the Black Cuillin so safe. One can hardly slip on it, it is so rough.'

'You've said a mouthful!' exclaimed Deborah. 'My fingers are nearly worn away!'

'How stupid of me! Of course you must have some gloves to wear,' said Angus, stopping and opening his rucksack and pulling out a selection of old leather gloves. 'Take your choice! What about you, Annette?'

But Annette didn't need gloves. Her balance (due, no doubt, to her ballet training) was so good that she skipped merrily from one point of rock to the next like a little mountain goat.

Climbing up scree slopes is a tedious business. For one step upwards they slid down three (or so Annette thought!), and the whole mass of stones slid down with them. They climbed abreast where they could, so as to avoid bringing the larger stones crashing down upon each other.

'There's no danger of falling,' Angus assured them when they stopped for a breather half way up, and stood looking back at the steep slope below them plunging down to the floor of the corrie. 'The scree cannot lie at a steeper angle than about forty-five degrees, so you couldn't fall very far, even if you wished. You would stop after a few yards or so.'

'I'll take your word for it,' panted Deborah. 'But right now I guess I'll just sit down where I am. It feels a whole lot safer!' She did so, and slid gently for a foot or two and then stopped.

'You see!' laughed Angus.

Annette, on the other hand, stood poised on the moving mountain-side, like a skier at the top of a 'run'.

'Oh, look, Angus! There's something down there.' They all looked where she pointed, and, sure enough, they caught sight of the antlers of a red deer. He stood on the lip of the corrie, sniffing the wind, and in a second or two galloped away.

'I expect he scented *you*, Deborah!' laughed Annette. 'I don't know what he would make of your French perfume. I expect he thought you were a very exotic sort of an animal!'

'I expect he caught sight of you standing there waving your arms about,' retorted Deborah. 'Oh, what a pity—we've lost sight of the castle and the loch. I liked to see them down below—it didn't seem quite so lonely.'

'We shall see them again from the top,' promised Angus. 'Always provided it is clear.'

It was from the top of Blaven that Annette had her first glimpse of the Black Cuillin. She stood there for a long time, quite silent, just looking at them. There they lay, a great grey-green stony horseshoe, immeasurably old and wrinkled, seamed with scars and fissures, crowned with fantastic spires and pinnacles. Even on this hot summer day the mists hung in the stony corries, and clung to the topmost peaks in tattered streamers. No blade of grass was there on these incredible mountains; no living thing moved on them. They looked as if they were made of metal, twisted by volcanic action into strange and weird shapes, or as if a demon from the Underworld, bent on mischief, had exploded a great charge of dynamite and shattered the grey mass into a range of splintered knife-edged peaks and razor-sharp pinnacles, and had then tired of his play, waved his wand and turned them all to stone.

'Ugh!' said Annette at length with a shiver. 'I'm not sure whether I like them. I think I'm frightened of them. They make me feel queer!'

'Many people have said that,' answered Angus. 'But when one has climbed them, one learns to love them too, though one is always just a little in awe of them, especially when one stands in such places as Coire Lagan and looks up at Sgurr Alasdair, rising into the sky in one tremendous leap. One feels very small amidst such grandeur.'

'I guess I'd like something to eat,' put in Deborah prosaically. 'Or better still, something to drink. Those mountains look so dry, they sure make me feel thirsty!'

'Lunch it is, then,' laughed Angus, 'It's after one o'clock. The others have stopped for lunch too.' He pointed across to the Clach Glas ridge where two tiny figures could be seen—Jaimie and Sheena.

'Gosh! I'm sure glad it's them and not me!' said Deborah. 'One mountain at a time is my motto. There's

108

no more strength left in my legs. Someone will just have to carry me home again, or I shall stay on the top of this mountain for the rest of my life!'

'You wait until supper-time,' teased Angus, 'You'll find the strength coming back to your legs all right!'

It was six o'clock when the two climbers returned. Sheena was obviously on top of the world—in every sense of the word. She had shown Jaimie that she was a climber worthy of his notice. Not once had she faltered. Where he had led, she had followed only a few feet behind. Edging round bastions of rock, 'backing up' chimneys, inching along narrow ledges, ascending, roped together, precipitous faces of rock where only experienced climbers could find the 'holds' for fingers, the tiny crevices for the feet. Yes, together they had conquered the peak and the dangerous pinnacles that lay between it and Blaven. A wonderful, wonderful day! thought Sheena, but she said nothing. And Jaimie thought it was a wonderful day too, though he had climbed this peak many times before. 'Perhaps,' he thought, 'this is the last time I shall ever climb it, and if so, how fitting that I should have such a companion.' At that moment he was full of admiration for Sheena. She was so beautiful, yet she was as tough as a man.

They ate the rest of their provisions, and then Angus stood up, stretched himself and said that they had better be leaving the mountain.

'But first we must have a last look at the view,' he exclaimed. 'Such a day as this we may never have again. It is indeed "white wander weather"!'

They found a good view-point, and stood looking out over Camasunnary Bay and Loch Scavaig, with the green island of Soay lying like an emerald in the blue sea. Beyond that lay Rhum, with its own Cuillin lightly veiled in a heat haze, and far, far out on the horizon floated the magic islands of the Outer Hebrides. Over to the right lay the ever-present dark ridge of the Black Cuillin.

'And now we must be descending,' said Jaimie in his turn. 'The sun is already beginning to go down, and although daylight lingers on the tops of the mountains it will be dusk by the time we are home.'

Oh, the fun they had skating down the scree slopes on

their heels! Annette managed to do it like an expert the very first time, but poor Deborah kept sitting down at intervals, and, as she said, it wasn't exactly like landing on a feather-bed.

They reached the stony corrie at last, and the roar of the waterfalls came to their ears. Soon they were over the lip of the corrie, and there, below them, looking so near you might drop a stone on it, lay Loch Slapin with Jaimie's boat drawn up on the shingle. They kept to the bank of the stream most of the way, and every now and then Annette kept stopping to pick a nosegay of the lovely little flowers that grew in sheltered hollows. Once, in a boggy place, they came upon a patch of the frail white flowers called Grass of Parnassus, and Annette had to stop and gather a bunch to tuck in her belt, and very wet she became in the process. The others sat on the edge of the bog and waited for her, and laughed when she fell in.

The last stretch of country was a couple of miles of spongy moorland, dotted with stones and boulders, and it was then that Annette realised once more the truth of Angus's words—that you must treat the mountains of Skye with respect as regards footwear. Squelching along in their big boots the party made a bee-line for the shore. None of them talked much—not even Deborah—they were all far too tired and hungry. Once Deborah's boot-lace came undone, and Angus stopped to tie it for her, for, as poor Deborah said, if she sat down she would certainly never get up again.

'Yes, it is a long walk to the top of Blaven, is it not?' said Angus, turning to look back at the mountain, 'although it looks so near.'

It was then that Annette knew what it was that made the way Angus spoke different from that of other people. And come to think of it, Jaimie too, and to a lesser degree Sheena. They all spoke very slowly and deliberately, and they didn't shorten their words by apostrophes. Angus had just said 'is it not?' whereas Annette would have said 'isn't it?'. But of course it was easy, said Annette to herself, to talk as if one had all the time in the world when one lived in a place like this, where one's days were governed by sunrises and sunsets and tides, instead of by buses and trains and wireless and alarm-clocks and the rush-hour. Here, one's thoughts just went on and on, and there were no motor cars (or so few they hardly counted) to hoot at you, or taxi-drivers to yell 'Hi! Look where you're going, missy! You'll be having a narsty accident, you will!' It might be argued that Annette herself had lived for the best part of her life in the depths of the country. Nowhere could possibly be more peaceful than Mintlaw. But then Annette had gone to school in the busy city of Newcastle, and besides, she was half French, so it was no wonder the words came tumbling out of her mouth so fast they tripped over themselves!

## Seeing Skye

OH, how the week sped away! They went in the car to Elgol on the Tuesday, and Annette saw the Black Cuillin from another angle—from the rocky shores of Loch Coruisk. Dark and forbidding, they rose in a stony amphitheatre, three hundred feet and more at one tremendous leap. Angus had gone with Jaimie on his rounds, so there were only the womenfolk in the boat— oh, and of course Pop. You almost forgot about Pop sitting silently in the bows.

'Well, can you beat it?' said Mamie Slaughter, examining the nearest mountain through her field-glasses. 'I declare they look just as if they were made of lead! What's the name of that mountain, boatman?'

'He is being called Sgurr na Stri,' answered Sandy Mac-Farlane dourly. Although he made quite a lot of money by rowing people like the Slaughters over to view Loch Coruisk, he still didn't approve of their doing it. 'He is not the highest one,' he added unnecessarily, seeing that Mamie had no idea at all about heights. 'He is being very easy to climb, and you are having a grand view from the top of him.' (As a matter of fact, this was all hearsay on Sandy's part, as he had never climbed the mountain himself, and would never have thought of doing so.) 'It is said that the view from the top of yon mountain is the best in the island—for the viewing of the loch, that is,

111

but,' he went on, 'I do not think that perhaps you would find him easy yourself. He is needing someone who is used to the hill walking.'

'I guess so!' said Mamie with a grimace. 'I think we'll be content to look at it from below.'

'And the other ones?' put in Annette, looking at the black horseshoe of shattered peaks surrounding the dark stretch of water. 'What are they called?'

Sandy reeled off such a succession of weird-sounding names that Deborah put her fingers in her ears. 'Stop! Stop! I can't bear it!'

'Just tell me the name of the big one in the middle,' begged Annette.

'He is named Sgurr a' Ghreadaidh*,' said Sandy, 'which means the Peak of the Mighty Winds, and to the right of it is Sgurr a' Madaidh,† the Foxes' Peak.'

'Well, I think their names are fascinating, even if they *are* a little gloomy to look at,' pronounced Annette.

'Gloomy?' echoed Sheena, who had been quite silent so far. 'I think they are the most beautiful mountains in the whole world. I love every one of them.' She glared at Annette, but Annette did not take up the challenge. She was wondering what Angus was doing at this moment, and also what thoughts went through Pop Slaughter's head as he sat gazing over the dark waters to the mountains beyond. Pop was certainly a bit of a puzzle. You didn't quite know what to make of him.

'Well, let's be going back,' said Mamie after a while. 'I suppose you don't know where we could get a soft drink?' She appealed to Sandy. 'Gosh, am I hot!' The sun was indeed beating upon their little boat as it bobbed up and down upon the water.

Sandy stared at her thoughtfully. A 'soft' drink? Now what would the lady be meaning by that? How could a drink be other than wet?

'My wife would make you a cup of tea maybe,' he said helpfully. 'She is good at the tea making is my wife.'

'Tea? Couldn't she turn out something cold?' said Mamie, fanning herself with the guide-book, *Seeing Skye*, from which she was never parted. 'Gosh, what would I give for an ice-cream soda, or even a glass of coca-cola!'

Sandy regarded her pityingly. Who but a mad American

* Pronounced, 'Hreeta'    † Pronounced, 'Vatee'

112

would be preferring a drink of lemonade to a cup of good strong black tea? (Tea is almost a national drink in the Highlands.)

'Och, then I am thinking you will have to drink out of the burn at the door,' he said with a shrug. 'The water in it will be cold enough for you, maybe.'


On the Wednesday they went to Dunvegan Castle and were shown all over it, not forgetting the famous dungeon into which the unfortunate prisoners of the MacLeods were thrown, and which were so near the dining-hall that the groans of the prisoners could be heard by the diners.

'Oh, how horrible! The poor, poor things!' exclaimed Annette with a shudder, as she looked down into the murky depths.

But Sheena's green eyes held no pity.

'Och, they would have done it themselves if they had been the conquerors,' she said with a shrug.

'Well, that sure is a mighty queer thing for a MacDonald to say,' commented Deborah. 'I sort of thought you two families were sworn enemies.'

'So we were,' answered Sheena, 'but that is not to say that we despised each other—or each other's dungeons. As a matter of fact we MacDonalds had a pretty good one of our own at Duntulm, into which many of the MacLeods were thrown. You shall see it tomorrow when we visit that part of the island. My ancestors were driven out of their ancient stronghold by the spirit of my ancestor, Donald Gorm, who haunted it.'

Annette thought of her words when, the following day, they sat on the grassy hillside below the ruined castle and listened to the waves sighing on the shingly shore. It wasn't hard to imagine the restless ghost of the wicked Donald pacing the galleries and passages of the gaunt building. Coming back along the coast road they passed Flodigarry House, where Flora MacDonald had lived, and, towering above, were the beetling precipices and weird pinnacles of the Quirang. Farther on, they crossed the grass to see the Kilt Rock, and the waterfall of Mealt, which falls to the boulder-strewn shore in one great fifty-foot leap. Farther on, the road passed beneath the cliffs of the Storr, at the foot of which stand the 'Old Man' and the smaller pinnacle, the 'Old Woman', giant land-

marks for miles around. Tired and hungry, they had a
very late tea at one of the Portree hotels before climbing
back into the car for their forty-mile drive home. Yes,
distances are dwarfed in Skye. Thirty or forty miles is a
mere nothing. Why, you often have to go as far as that
round a loch to get to a place on the other side, only half
a mile or so away as the crow flies.

'What a pity we aren't crows, isn't it?' said Annette
sleepily. 'What a day we've had!'

'Didn't I tell you we'd show you Skye,' said Deborah
triumphantly. Unseen, Sheena's lips curled. Poor things—
they really thought they were seeing Skye! Well, thought
the Scottish girl, there are two ways of seeing things—with
your eyes and with your mind, and Skye was one of the
places you had to see with your mind, otherwise you didn't
really see it at all. And of course she was perfectly right.
Annette, standing on the top of Blaven, had (with a bit of
help from Angus) caught a glimpse of the real Skye, but
Mamie and Deborah only saw what the guide books told
them—namely, that 'Skye is an island with a thousand-
mile coastline, much indented by sea-lochs. The natives
of the island are poor and thriftless, much preferring to
stand at the doors of their cottages instead of working for
a living.' But the guide-books never mentioned the difficulty of cultivating land so stony that no modern methods
could be used, nor did they say where the poor natives
were to get the money from to buy the modern implements,
nor how to stop the young people from drifting over to the
mainland in order to earn a living. Why, here was Jaimie
Gordon, the laird of Airdrochnish himself, being forced to
leave his home, though it was nearly breaking his heart
to do.

## The ' Ceilidh '

YES, the week passed by all too quickly, and already
it was Friday, the day of the *ceilidh* at Ardavasar.
Jaimie and Angus had tea at the castle because
they were all going in the Slaughters' car, since Jaimie's

own small one was in 'dry dock', having a new engine put in. It was queer, thought Annette, to see Jaimie politely waiting to be asked to sit down in his own castle hall! She wondered what he thought about it, but his sombre face was quite inscrutable. If he minded being a guest in his own ancestral home he didn't show it. She would have got a shock if she could have looked into the young man's heart at that moment, and seen just how much it rebelled at the sight of the Slaughters' rose-strewn stair-carpet, the many oil-stoves, the tartan curtains (the wrong tartan!)—yes, even the Slaughters themselves, though he knew quite well that this was illogical and that he ought to be grateful to them. Indeed, he would be in a much worse position without them and their American dollars.

'Do have a scone, Mr Gordon' (Mamie still went on calling him 'mister', thinking it too familiar to use his Christian name). 'Mairi is ever so good at making them, and she's getting us quite used to your English tea—I should really say Scottish, shouldn't I? Oh, but of course I keep on forgetting that Mairi is your own servant.'

'Not my servant,' corrected Jaimie seriously. 'Mairi is my kinswoman and she sometimes comes here—when I am living here, I mean—and does a little work for me, but she is not taking any money for it. When her cow is ill I attend her for nothing, and so we manage very well.'

As Mamie Slaughter said afterwards, you couldn't make head nor tail of the laird. You'd be sorry for him, but his quiet dignity forbade it. Indeed, sometimes you had an idea he was feeling sorry for *you*, which was just plain ridiculous.

After tea they went to get ready for the *ceilidh*. Angus and Jaimie got 'all dressed up', as Annette put it, in kilts, velvet jackets, lace cravats and tartan stockings. Sheena wore the kilt too, because the three of them, with Elspeth MacLeod making a fourth, were going to give an exhibition of Highland dancing for the benefit of any visitors who were still here after the Skye Gathering. Everyone for miles around who had any talent had been roped in for the occasion, and it was said that this was to be a *ceilidh* of *ceilidhs*! It was rumoured that there was to be a real ballet-dancer (someone who had danced at the Gathering Ball at Portree last Saturday, a girl called Annette Dancy) to show them what dancing is like in England. Yes,

115

Annette herself had promised to do her bit, and she was dancing a *solo* from *Giselle*.

'At least I will if I can get a frock from somewhere, or a bit of something to make one with,' she said, looking thoughtfully at the Slaughter curtains. But alas, all the curtains in the castle were tartan—not a lace one amongst them—and you couldn't dance a *solo* from *Giselle* in a tartan curtain, could you?

'Well, what about an ordinary dance dress?' Mamie had said. 'Sheena would lend you her white one, wouldn't you, honey? It's "ballet length" as they say over here, so it would be fine for you to dance in.'

'I sent it home last Monday,' Sheena answered smoothly. 'It was really so dirty I thought it ought to go to the cleaners.'

'Oh, but that can't be the one Momma means,' put in Deborah. 'I saw the white one she's talking about hanging in the clothes-closet only jest this morning. Or perhaps you've made a mistake and sent the wrong one to the cleaners instead.'

'It is you who have made the mistake, I think,' said Sheena. 'You must have been dreaming.' And sure enough, when Deborah had looked in the wardrobe soon afterwards, no glistening white frock hung there. She might have found it, however, if she had looked a little farther—in Sheena's suitcase—but being Deborah she never thought of doing so.

But to get back to the frock. In the end Annette had been fitted out with an old one of Deborah's. It was made of pale green net, and they had shortened it so that she was able to dance without tripping up. And lovely she looked in it! The strange thing was that the moment Annette put on a ballet-dress she was immediately transformed from a rather dowdily dressed (though always graceful) schoolgirl into an attractive *ballerina*.

At half past seven all six of them piled into the big Slaughter car (Pop was excused because there wasn't room for him), and soon they were speeding swiftly away from Airdrochnish towards Broadford, near where the road leading to the southern peninsula of Sleat branched off from the main one. It was a beautiful moonlight night, with not a cloud in the sky. 'At least, just a few little ones piling up on the horizon,' said Annette. 'I thought at

116

first that they were mountains. There always seem to be mountains on the horizon here in Skye.'

'I have been looking at those clouds,' said Jaimie, sitting on the front seat with Sheena and Murdo, who was driving as usual. 'I think that the weather is going to break. Those clouds mean wind.'

'Oh, *no*!' exclaimed Mamie. 'Why, it's a lovely night. I think it's set fine for ages.' The weather during the past week had been so lovely that it had almost reconciled Mamie to the island. She declared she'd be almost sorry to leave it!

At this point they were passing Duisdale House, and a little farther on Jaimie pointed out a dark lonely lochan, with water-lilies shining upon it, and Grass of Parnassus growing in silvery patches on its banks.

'That is Loch nan Dubhrachan,' he told them. 'It is another of Skye's haunted lochs—the most famous one. Yes, it is quite certain that a terrible water-horse dwells in its depths, and one day the inhabitants are dragging the loch for him, and the water-horse is catching the drag in his teeth and holding it fast. They are so frightened that they are all running away. Indeed it is so!'

'I'll bet it got caught in the weeds on the bottom,' laughed Deborah. But the two Scotsmen didn't join in the laughter.

'There were his hoof-marks on the shore the next morning,' put in Murdo, in support of his lord and master. 'So that will be convincing you, I hope, that what the laird says is true.'

Glancing at the laird's dark face, Annette couldn't decide whether he really believed in his island's fairy stories or not. She thought he probably did, and Angus too!

All roads led to Ardavasar that night! As they emerged from the Armadale woods and took the stony road leading to the little village, they passed groups of people on foot and several other cars all going in the same direction. The *ceilidh* was well under way when they got there, and as they drew near to the tiny hall they could hear the tinkle of a piano and the sound of a voice singing a strange sad Gaelic song.

Inside the hall the *ceilidh* was proceeding in a very orderly manner, due, no doubt, to the fact that the local policeman was acting as M.C.! A young man in full Highland dress was playing the piano on the platform, whilst another (equally gloriously attired) was singing the song they had heard from outside. They were followed by a row of solemn-faced school children (awe-stricken by the important occasion), who also sang in their native tongue. After this they danced a Highland Fling, which made the tiny platform rock and creak. Then came another song, this time by three girls dressed in kilts and white blouses.

And so it went on, until nearly everyone had contributed in some way towards the entertainment. The benches had been pushed back, Jaimie and his companions had danced their exhibition reels, and the applause had nearly taken the roof off. Besides being a brilliant dancer the young laird was a popular figure. Annette had given of her best in her *Giselle* solo and they had clapped politely, though it was clear that, like the inhabitants of Fort William, they found classical ballet a little hard to understand. Still they appreciated the 'turned out' position of legs and feet, for, strangely enough, Scottish dancing depends on this position too.

And now it was Sheena's turn to sing. She began with a setting of Adexander Smith's poem, *Oh, Blaven, rocky Blaven*, that she had sung in the car the night Annette had arrived. Then she gave them a sad little Gaelic song about a Skyeman leaving his native island for a foreign land.

> 'Glendounie, O Glendounie,' sang Sheena,
> ' 'Tis my soul that bids goodbye
> To the cottage by the sea-shore
> Where the many waters sigh.

> 'Glendounie, O Glendounie,
> 'Tis my heart that breaks in twain
> For the sheiling of my childhood
> I shall never see again.'

Jaimie, standing in the shadow of the doorway, heard in Sheena's soft husky voice all his own misery. . . .

> 'Glendounie, O Glendounie . . .'

And then, so that they should not all be crying because of the sadness of her song, the girl gave them, as an encore:

118

'A Gordon for me! A Gordon for me!
If you're no a Gordon, you're no use to me!'

With one voice they all joined in the chorus, and the
little hall fairly rocked with the old favourite, and much
chaffing did the young laird receive, for was he not a
Gordon himself and the lassie who sang the song a bonny
one!

A little after midnight Jaimie and Sheena went out into
the dark night to get a breath of fresh air. The clouds were
by now beginning to cover the sky, and a cold little wind
was getting up. More and more people had crowded into
the *ceilidh*, and the hotter it got, the more they seemed to
enjoy themselves.

'Where did you find the song you sang this evening?'
asked Jaimie, as they walked side by side up the stony
road. 'The one about Glendounie? I do not remember
hearing it before.'

'I made it up myself,' answered Sheena. 'Glendounie is
my village.'

'I am knowing that,' said Jamie. 'It seemed to me that
you were singing about yourself.'

'That is true,' answered Sheena. 'This evening I have
felt that I may go away from Glendounie to another
country.'

If Jamie felt surprised at this statement he didn't show it.
Instead he asked, 'Oh, and how will that be happening?'

'You may have noticed some visitors at the *ceilidh*,'
went on Sheena.

'There were many visitors,' said Jamie. 'I have counted
at least twenty people whom I do not know. Some of them
are visitors who have stayed on here after the Gathering.'

'Two of them—the men in evening dress—were from
the hotel at Armadale,' said Sheena. 'You have noticed
them?'

'Yes, I have noticed them,' said the young man. His tone
told her nothing.

'One of these men is a talent scout,' Sheena told him.
'You know that a company of Celtic dancers are to go to
Canada shortly?'

'I have heard something about it.'

'Well, this man is finding Scottish dancers to make up
the company. He talked to me, and, in short, if I attend

119

an audition that is to be held in the Gathering Hall in Portree on Monday afternoon, I shall be given a place. He as good as promised me, only he cannot make it definite until I have been to the audition.'

'And the other man?' asked Jaimie politely.

'Och, the other man—he has something to do with a film they are making in the island.'

'A film?'

'Yes, but I do not know its name. Anyhow, it has nothing to do with me,' said Sheena.

Jaimie didn't answer, but had Sheena been able to see his eyes at that moment she would have been struck by the expression in them. Mamie Slaughter was right when she said that 'the laird was a dark one'!


## What Happened To Pop?

WHEN they came out of the *ceilidh*, which wasn't until two o'clock in the morning, the little bank of cloud had spread over the whole sky, covering the moon. The rain lashed against the double windows of Airdrochan Casle, the wind rose and shrieked in its twisted chimneys. Annette was far too tired and slept too soundly to hear it, but next morning when she woke it was to find a different Skye from the lovely blue and golden island she had known during the last few days. Out of her window she could see nothing but swirling clouds of mist, now hiding, now revealing the jagged black peaks of Clach Glas. Placid Loch Slapin was whipped into white-capped waves, the grove of stunted trees sheltering the castle from the north were bent low against the wind, and the rain slanted down relentlessly in a steel-grey curtain. You could hardly believe it was the same place as yesterday.

It was late when Annette went down to breakfast, but she found nobody in the dining-room, so evidently her hosts were still in bed, and were probably having breakfast there. Making her way down the many cold stone passages to the kitchen to tell Mairi that she was down and wanting her breakfast, she found that damsel in the middle of reciting what was evidently a very dramatic story to Donald Gordon's children (all six of them, for, as it was Saturday, none of them were at school).

'Aye,' continued Mairi, changing quickly from the Gaelic to the English as Annette appeared in the doorway, 'it iss being a very terrible storm.' (Extra 's's' crept into Mairi's words when she became excited, and the present tense took the place of the less dramatic past.) 'I am looking out of my kitchen window, and the great tree iss falling. Yes—right across the path it is falling! You should have heard the crash and the splintering. I am nearly dropping the porridge-pan that I am holding, and the porridge in it too!'

'Goodness!' exclaimed Annette, running over to the window where, sure enough, she could see the great tree (the only really big one in Airdrochnish) lying across the causeway. 'What a blessing nobody was underneath it when it fell! Did the children see it?'

'Och, no, puir bairnies,' cried Mairi. 'They are being far too busy rubbing the sleep out of their eyes to see it! No-one except Mairi iss seeing the great tree fall.' (Privately Annette wondered if Mairi had really seen it herself, or if she was only making it up to feel important; but if so, it was clear that she was rapidly making herself believe she had done so.) 'But what a good thing,' she went on, 'that Murdo and the master were away to the fishing before it came down. Only a few minutes it was, too.'

'W-what did you say, Mairi?' stammered Annette, hardly able to believe her ears. '*Fishing?* You don't mean —you can't mean that Poppa Slaughter has gone out *fishing?*'

'Yes, indeed,' declared Mairi. 'This morning early he is taking the car, and he and Murdo are away to the fishing, rods and everything, and the long mackintosh boots, and both of them grinning like I don't know what. Never have I seen the master smile before, and as for Murdo he would give his soul to go to the fishing.'

She was talking to the empty air, for Annette had already dashed out of the kitchen, back along the many passages, and up to Mamie Slaughter's bedroom. She found her hostess propped up in bed with a tartan cloak over the top of her marabout-trimmed jacket, and an extra oil-stove between her and the window. She was reading a letter, and it was clear to Annette that in it was the news that she herself had just heard. Her mouth had dropped open, and the astonished expression on her face almost made Annette burst out laughing.

'W-aal! What d'you know! Poppa's gone fishing! See here what he says.'

*Have been doing a bit of hard thinking while you folks were at the what-d'you-call-it, and have come to the conclusion that since I bought the automobile with dollars earned by myself, it's only just right and proper that I should be able to take a ride in it when I want to. I have discovered a kindred soul in Murdo, and we have gone fishing. No women needed on this trip—no, sir! We shall probably (but not certainly) return in a few weeks' time. Until then I trust you will be able to amuse yourselves without*

*Your devoted (but liberated) Poppa.*

'W-aal!' exclaimed Mamie again. ' "A few weeks' time", he says. A few weeks, and no automobile! Can you beat it?'

'As a matter of fact, it wouldn't have mattered if we *had* had the car,' said Annette soothingly, 'because a huge tree has fallen down right across the drive.'

'A tree?' said Mamie. 'My! My! It never rains but it pours!' (which was truer than she realised—in Skye, anyway!) 'All last night I lay awake thinking my last minute had come. . . . Oh, here's Debbie. Take a look at this, Deb.' She held out the note. 'Poppa's gone fishing.'

Deborah wasn't quite as astonished or taken aback as her mother.

'W-aal, good for Pop!' she said when she had read the letter. 'Here's hoping he catches lots of fish! I felt a bit guilty about poor old Poppa, sitting there, saying jest nothin'. It's sure time he had a break.'

'But what are we going to do without the car?' asked Mamie.

'We'll jest have to walk on our own two feet, like everyone else in this place,' said Deborah. 'Maybe we'll see a whole lot more.' (Which showed that Deborah, at least, had caught a little of the spirit of the island.) 'By the way,' she added, 'where's Sheena? She's not in her room.'

Nobody had seen Sheena. She had evidently got up and gone out early. Where she could have gone to in the wind and the rain was a mystery. But then Sheena herself was a bit of an enigma, they all felt. As a matter of fact Sheena had wakened early and, hearing the tumult of the storm, had got up, dressed quickly and gone out. She walked for several miles, right round the head of the loch, and across the rough moorland towards Coire Uaigneich, revelling in the wildness all around her, the low clouds boiling in the corrie as though in a cauldron, the mist driving across the scarred face of Blaven, the shining curtain of rain, now hiding, now revealing, the awful peaks of Clach Glas, the roar of many waterfalls.

It was after ten o'clock when she walked back up the causeway and found, to her amazement, her way barred by the fallen tree. Standing beside it was Seumas, the postman, with his bicycle. You might have thought he would have left it at home in such weather, but that was not Seumas's way. A bicycle was of no use to him now, it is true, but who could tell when the storm might not abate? There was more sound sense in his reasoning than might at first appear. The weather can change with lightning rapidity in Skye.

Sheena greeted the old man in the Gaelic which made his rugged face light up.

'I have delivered the letters up at the castle this morning,' he said, 'and then a telegram is coming by telephone from London. We are trying to send it on the telephone to the castle, but there is no answer. At first we do not know what to think, and then we are hearing about the tree coming down, and all the telephone wires with it. So I am bringing it myself before I go up to Strathbeg.'

'Let me take it for you,' offered Sheena, holding out her hand. 'I'm just going back there now.'

'I am thanking you, Miss Sheena,' said old Seumas gratefully. 'That will be of great benefit to me, as I am late already. It is taking me a very long time to deliver the letters in such weather. You will be careful with the telegram for the lassie. Yes, as you see, it is for the English girl, and it is to tell her to go back to London at once, so you see it is very important.'

'I'll see to it,' promised Sheena. 'We shall have to get someone to saw up the tree and move it,' she added, putting the orange envelope into the pocket of her mackintosh. 'It is urgent, because on Monday I shall want Murdo to drive me to Broadford in the car, where I can get a bus to Portree, unless he wishes to drive me the whole way.'

'You are forgetful that today is Saturday and a half-day for the woodmen,' said Seumas impassively, 'and the morrow it is the Sabbath Day. You will not be getting anyone to move yon tree until the Monday, I am thinking."

'But it *must* be moved!' exclaimed Sheena. 'It must! It must, you stupid old man!'

'I am not being as stupid as some other people are being,' said Seumas with dignity. 'If the tree is being moved now, this very minute, there is no motor car to drive you anywhere.'

For a moment Sheena said nothing out of sheer amazement.

"No car?' she burst out at length. 'Whatever do you mean?'

Leisurely, and with the Gaelic sense of drama, old Seumas proceeded to tell the astonished girl all about Poppa Slaughter, Murdo, and the fishing trip, all of which had been told to *him* in the first place by Elspeth, Murdo's wife.

'And no-one is knowing where they have gone, or when they are returning,' he added triumphantly (stupid old man, indeed!), 'not even Elspeth herself.'

Then it suddenly dawned upon Sheena what a plight she was in. The Slaughters' car had disappeared into the vast emptiness of Skye, vanished without a trace. Jaimie's car was out of commission. How was she to get to Broadford to catch her bus? Then an idea came to her (she was a native of this island, remember, and people who live on remote islands are ever resourceful).

'Oh, Seumas,' she begged, 'I'm in such a *dreadful* fix. That was why I called you stupid—I was at my wits' end. I didn't really mean it. Seumas, you simply must help me.'

'And how am I able to be helping you, Miss Sheena,' said Seumas stiffly.

'You must lend me your bicycle,' said Sheena. 'Oh, I don't mean now, but on Monday. It's much too far for me to walk all the way to Broadford when I have to dance

"Oh, Seumas," she begged, "I'm in such a dreadful fix."

afterwards, but if I had your bicycle I could do it. Oh, please, please. Seumas.'

Seumas looked at her severely. She had called him a stupid old man, but she had apologised. Moreover, she was a bonny lassie with her auburn hair blowing in the wind—Seumas had a weakness for red hair—and her strange green eyes. Besides, (and this was even more important in Seumas's eyes) she was his kinswoman.

'You are welcome, Miss Sheena,' he said at length, 'but you will have to be walking to Strathbeg for the machine. I am not walking there myself for you or ony other lassie i' the Isle. My legs are not being as strong as they once were.'

'Oh, thank you, thank you!' said Sheena. "And of course I'll walk over to Strathbeg for the bicycle. That will be nothing at all—only a couple of miles. I'll ride it back to Strathbeg for you at night and walk from there home myself. I promise faithfully.'

'Och, then, in that case ye can borrow the machine,' answered Seumas with a shrug. (Which goes to show the heights Highland kinship will scale.) 'And I am wishing you luck in your audition, or whatever it is they call it.' Then he added as an afterthought, 'I do not hold wi' dancin' awa' to them foreign parts masel'.' All this talk between them had taken place out in the wind and the rain, but for all the notice they took of it the sun might have been shining.

When Seumas had turned and was wheeling his bicycle back down the causeway, Sheena took the telegram out of her pocket and stared at it jealously. It was important, was it? It was to tell Annette to go back to London so that she might get the chief part in some ballet or other? Well, there was always 'the slip 'twixt cup and lip', wasn't there? To-day was Saturday. Tomorrow was the Sabbath Day . . . She put the envelope back into her pocket.

It was at this moment that Jaimie came through the door in the wall leading out of the courtyard. He had evidently been up to the castle for his letters which were left there for him every morning. He did not exclaim in horror at the sight of Sheena's dripping hair and wet clothes—it did not seem at all extraordinary to him, living as he had done, all his life, in this wet island.

'Good morning,' he said. 'Had Seumas forgotten some-

126

thing?' (Oh, then he had seen the old man? Sheena's mind worked quickly.)

'Oh, no,' she said. 'He came to have a look at the tree. Have you seen it, Jaimie? It has fallen right across the causeway. It is fortunate, as Seumas said, that Poppa Slaughter and Murdo were not underneath it. It must have come down only five minutes after they went down the drive.'

'Yes, I am seeing it,' answered Jaimie. 'I must be arranging to have it moved, but that can wait until Monday, I think. Tomorrow, being the Sabbath Day, no-one will be needing to use the causeway, now that the Slaughters' car is not here.'

'Talking about cars,' put in Sheena, 'I suppose yours is not finished yet?'

'No,' said Jaimie. 'It will be Tuesday or Wednesday before the new engine is in.'

'What a pity,' observed Sheena. 'I was going to ask you to take me to Portree to my audition on Monday. It is going to be a little difficult for me to get there.'

'It is fortunate, then, that my car is out of commission,' said Jaimie, 'for that saves argument. I am not sure that I would have taken you to Portree in it, even if the new engine were in.'

Sheena was silent for a moment, wondering what he meant by this.

'Why not?' she said at length.

'I am thinking that your place is here in the island,' said Jaimie. 'Too many young people are leaving the island.'

'But you're leaving it yourself,' exclaimed Sheena, struck with the lack of logic in his reasoning.

'You do not think, do you, that I would leave the island if it were not for sheer necessity?' said Jaimie sombrely. 'You know, surely, that it is breaking my heart to do so, but I am a man and I have my living to make.'

'What about me?' cried Sheena. 'What is there for me to do here—unless you want me to keep sheep!'

'There are other things that a woman can do,' observed Jaimie. 'I do not think that it is at all fitting for Sheena MacDonald of Glendounie to go away to be a professional dancer.'

'You sound like old Seumas!' exclaimed Sheena, her temper rising. ' "I do not hold wi' dancin' awa' to them

127

foreign parts masel'. . . ." But at least Seumas cared
enough for me to offer me the loan of his precious bicycle
on Monday to get me to Broadford so that I can catch a
bus to Portree.'

'Perhaps I am caring for you too much to help you in
that way,' said Jaimie gravely.

'Well, what would you have me do?' demanded Sheena,
looking up at him from beneath her eyelashes on which
the raindrops glistened.

'That I shall tell you in my own good time,' said Jaimie.
'Or it may be that I shall never tell you at all.' He did not
explain further, but made her his stiff little bow and strode
away down the causeway, leaving her staring after him.

## Sunday in Skye

ALL that Saturday the storm raged. The wind flung
itself against the windows of the castle and the rain
streamed down the leaded panes. Mamie Slaughter
sat in her bedroom, surrounded by oil-stoves, and wrapped
in tartan cloaks. Deborah wrote letters to her friends back
home, whilst Annette wrote to her mother. Sheena went
out into the storm, and returned, wet to the skin, but with
shining eyes and a faint rose colour whipped into her pale
cheeks. Angus came in after tea, and they played Charades
in the castle hall, which made a grand setting for drama.
Jaimie called later on, and stood silently watching them as
they acted the word 'peregrinator'—a scene of Bonnie
Prince Charlie's wanderings throughout the Island of Skye
—and if he thought it strange that a crowd of Sassenachs
should be acting a scene which might well have taken
place in this very castle, he did not say so.

Next morning the mist had lifted a little, though it was
still raining. Out of her bedroom window Annette could
see the silver thread of the waterfall in Coire Uaigneich,
swollen to a great white ribbon of foam. You could hear its
dull roar across the water. The jagged black peaks of
Clach Glas were tipped with white. Snow! Yes, it was
September, and Skye was reminding you that winter was
only just round the corner!

As usual on the Sabbath Day Mamie Slaughter breakfasted in bed, but Deborah was up, and she and Annette were just beginning their porridge when Sheena walked in. In her hand she held an orange envelope.

'There's a telegram for you, Annette,' she said, holding it out. 'Seumas has just brought it. He said it came late last night by telephone but there was no-one to send it with.'

Annette seized the envelope and read it quickly.

'I do hope it is not bad news?' said Sheena smoothly.

'It's to tell me that our ballet, *La Sylphide*, is to be in a Scottish film that they are making,' answered Annette. 'And I'm to go back to London immediately. Paddy says—it's Paddy who has sent the wire—that I may get a part in the *corps de ballet* if I show up. Of course Simonetta is to dance the chief rôle—I couldn't expect to have that, of course—but I ought to get a place in the *corps*, if only I can get there in time for the audition. It's on Monday night—that's tomorrow—on stage, after the show. I *must* get there in time. If I get a train from the mainland tonight I ought to just do it. I ought to get paid very well if I'm in a film, don't you think, even just in the *corps de ballet*, and the extra money will make all the difference to my mother. Where can I get a train from?' She appealed to Deborah. 'Do you think your mother would let Murdo take me to the ferry? Oh, but I'm forgetting—there isn't any car, or any Murdo.'

'You are forgetting something else too,' put in Sheena. 'It is the Sabbath Day.'

At first Annette didn't realise the full import of this statement, but when she did she gave a positive wail of anguish.

'You mean—you mean——'

'I mean that there is no ferry functioning, so the car would have been no use to you, even if it had been there; and in any case you would never have persuaded Murdo to go joy-riding on the Sabbath Day,' declared Sheena.

'It isn't joy-riding,' cried Annette. 'It's my work.'

'Oh, well it is all the same, isn't it?' insisted Sheena. '"Thou shalt do no work on the Sabbath Day", you know. Of course I am being very sorry for you, Annette, but after all it cannot be helped, can it?'

'It *must* be helped!' cried Annette, jumping up from the

table and leaving her porridge half eaten. 'I can't just sit here and do nothing. Oh, why, *why* couldn't the telegram have come yesterday! I could have *walked* to the ferry.'

'It's rather a long way, honey,' put in Deborah. 'Couldn't you wait till tomorrow morning and we'll send to Broadford for a car?'

'Oh, Debbie, it's sweet of you to think of it, but tomorrow will be too late, don't you see,' said Annette.

'Wouldn't they put off the audition?'

Annette sighed at the ignorance of the general public where the stage is concerned.

'They just *don't* put off auditions,' she answered. 'Especially for a mere member of the *corps de ballet*. If you're there you get in, if you're lucky; if you aren't—well, that's the end as far as you're concerned. You've "had it", as you would say, Deb. I've simply *got* to get there somehow. There must be a way. I'm going to see Angus. Angus will know what to do. And there's Jaimie as well. Jaimie's so sweet—he'll help me.'

Any qualms of conscience Sheena might have were stifled by this speech. Jaimie sweet, indeed! What right had Annette Dancy to call Jaimie sweet, or to ask him to help her?

'I am afraid you will find that even Jaimie will be unable to alter the Scottish Sabbath,' she said. 'And really, Annette, you *would* come here, so in a way it's all your own fault.'

But Annette had already dashed out into the hall, snatched up a mackintosh, crammed her feet into a pair of shoes that happened to be standing there, and had let herself out into the wet morning.

By great good luck she found both Jaimie and Angus at home. They had finished the chores and were now preparing to go off climbing (yes, the weather made no difference at all to these tough young men, though they would not have allowed a girl to accompany them on their expedition). Angus gave an exclamation of surprise when he saw Annette in her flapping mackintosh (she hadn't stopped to fasten the buttons), and her white tragic face.

'Annette!' he exclaimed, stopping in the middle of lacing up his climbing boots. 'Is something the matter?'

'Yes—oh, yes—the most terrible thing has happened,'
130

panted Annette. 'This morning Seumas brought me a telegram. . . .' Breathlessly she explained everything—all about the film, and the ballet, the necessity of her getting to London by tomorrow night. 'But, as Sheena says, it's the Sabbath Day, and there are no taxis, no ferries, no *anything*,' she concluded dramatically. 'Oh, Angus—oh, Jaimie —what am I to do?'

What indeed? The two young men looked at each other. How, short of flying like a bird, could one get from Skye over to the mainland on the Sabbath Day?

'It is most unfortunate that the telegram should have come only this morning,' said Angus. 'If it had come yesterday it might have been possible to do something.'

'Well, actually Sheena said it came last night by telephone,' said Annette, 'but there was no-one to bring it up to the castle. Anyway I couldn't have done anything late last night, could I?'

'Sheena said?' echoed Jaimie, speaking for the first time. 'What has Sheena to do with this telegram?'

'She met old Seumas bringing it up this morning,' explained Annette. 'Oh, if only, if only it had come *yesterday* morning.'

'Yes, it would certainly have been easier,' admitted Jaimie. 'Still, we must not give up. Transport must be found.'

'But even if we *did* get some transport, there is no ferry service running,' said Annette. 'Sheena said so.'

'Hush you!' commanded Jaimie. 'You must not be listening to everything that a bit of a lassie like Sheena MacDonald is telling you. I think I know how it can be done. Wait you here, and I will go into the village and see what can be arranged.'

'I shall come too,' said Annette quickly.

'Have you had your breakfast?' asked Angus, knowing Annette and her impetuous ways.

'No, I forgot all about it when the telegram came,' she admitted.

'I thought as much! Well, while Jaimie is gone, you and I will make some porridge for you,' insisted Angus. 'You shall have it without salt, and with sugar and cream if you wish, but you are not going anywhere without your breakfast.'

'That is right,' said Jaimie with a nod of approval. 'Great

adventures must always be undertaken after a good breakfast. That is the climbers' rule!'

So saying, he went out of the cottage, and Annette and
Angus were left to make the porridge. They had just finished eating it when he returned. Annette saw by his face
that he had been successful, and her eyes began to dance.

'I can see you've managed something! I can see it! How
wonderful!'

'Not so fast!' answered Jaimie. 'While you finish your
bread and marmalade and drink up your tea, I will explain
my plan to Angus. It is a plan which I think will work, but
it is of much difficulty. You see, the telephone wires have
been brought down with the storm—oh, not only the castle
one (we are knowing that already) but the whole line is
out of order. It has not been working since yesterday
noon.' (His dark eyes met Angus's blue ones over the top
of Annette's head. 'How then had a telegram come from
London late last night?' said their glance. In very fact,
Jaimie had already found out exactly what had happened.)
'So,' he went on, 'it is not possible to ring up and get a
private car from Broadford, as I had hoped.'

'But you have a plan?' broke in Annette. 'You said you
had.' All the intrigue about telephone wires, telegrams and
the perfidious Sheena passed over her head. She had only
one thought—how to get to London in time.

'Yes, I have a plan,' answered Jaimie. 'I have arranged
for you to borrow old Seumas MacDonald's bicycle. He
is away on the hill with his sheep, but the bicycle is in his
cottage. He will not ride it himself on the Sabbath Day,
but Effie, his wife, says you may borrow it—if you care to
take the risk.'

If Annette hadn't been so perturbed she would have
laughed. As if God would be angry just because you rode
a bicycle on Sunday! But neither Jaimie nor Angus saw
anything the least queer about it.

'Now this is what you must do,' went on Jaimie. He
went over to a cupboard and pulled out a rucksack, and
from it a map. 'The two of you must ride to Broadford
on the bicycle, and when you are there you must try to get
a car to take you down the Glen Arroch road to the Kylerhea ferry. Oh, yes, I know that the ferry is not running,' he
explained as Annette began to break in, 'but the ferryman,
Dougal MacIntyre, is a friend of mine. He has a rowing-

boat, and if you give him my name I am thinking that he will take you across the narrows in it, or, if not, then he will lend it to you for you to row yourselves across. When you are on the far shore you must go to Sandy MacPhee's cottage—Dougal will be pointing it out to you from the boat, or from the Skye shore. Sandy will lend you a pony—he is having a wee Shetland one that will carry the lassie. . . .' All this time he had been pointing out the route to Angus, and showing him the difficulties. Angus nodded his head.

'With the help of the pony,' continued Jaimie, 'you must get round the coast from Glenelg. There is a road, but you cannot afford the time to go that way if you wish to get to Arnisdale before nightfall. Instead you must take the stony track past Loch à Ghleannain—you must be careful of the bogs here—passing between Meall Buidhe and Beinn Mhialàiridh. Here the path rises to over a thousand feet and is very rough indeed. After passing Loch na Lochain and beneath the lower slopes of Ben Sgriol,* you will descend until you come to the woods. After leaving these you will again join the road, and after a few miles of comparatively easy going you will come to Arnisdale, where a kinsman of mine lives. His name is Andrew Gordon, and he has a motor launch and will take you across the loch to Mallaig. The crossing will take you several hours, as there is a good stretch of open sea and the mouth of Loch Nevis to be negotiated, so, unless you get to Arnisdale sooner than I expect, it may be as well for you to stay the night there with Andrew and his wife and cross over in the morning in time to catch the 7.42 train from Mallaig to Fort William and Glasgow. We shall hope you will be in time to catch the afternoon train from Edinburgh to King's Cross. As far as I can see, this is the only chance of you getting to London by tomorrow night,' he added, straightening himself and turning to Annette. 'If you were to wait here until tomorrow morning, and if it were possible to get you to the Kyle ferry where you could catch a train to Inverness, I am still thinking that you would not arrive in London that night.'

Gravely Angus followed his directions on the map, making notes on the margin of Jaimie's kinsmen and friends,

* Pronounced, Skreel

133

where they lived, and any other information he thought might be of help to them on their journey.

'I would be coming with you,' said Jaimie, 'but I am thinking that the two of you will be faster than three, and besides,' he added, 'I have an idea that it is Angus who will like to be helping you.'

'Yes indeed, that is so,' said Angus.

While Annette finished her breakfast, Angus stuffed his rucksack with all manner of things—mackintoshes, woollies, food, maps, besides all the things that were already in it. Jaimie rummaged in his drawers for things for Annette to wear, even finding a pair of boots small enough for her when stuffed with socks. Although at the moment the rain had stopped, it still looked very threatening.

'There is no time to lose,' he said, when he had found what he wanted. 'You had better change into these things and pack your own clothes in Angus's rucksack, then you will not be needing to go back to the castle. You would only waste a lot of precious time in explanations. I shall tell the Slaughters what has happened, and you can write yourself when you get back to London and make your apologies for such an abrupt leave-taking. They are such very kind people that I am sure they will understand.'

## The Road from the Isle

WHEN Annette thought about their journey afterwards, she felt like comparing it with Bonnie Prince Charlie's wanderings over much the same ground. 'But of course,' she would add, 'he was Someone Terribly Important, with a price upon his head, and enemy soldiers lying in wait for him at every turn of the path, whereas *our* enemy was time, and, of course, the awful weather.' Yes, it made quite an amusing story to tell to her friends, but while it was happening it wasn't amusing at all.

It started well enough. Jaimie went with them to the MacDonald's cottage and saw them off. Seumas's wife,

134

Effie, gave them a packet of freshly baked scones and wished them good luck, although Annette could see she didn't approve of riding 'the machine', as she called it, on the Lord's Day. Seumas, himself, had just gone off to Strathbeg, so they didn't see him, but all the MacDonald children (there were eight of them) ran alongside as Angus rode away, with Annette perched on the step behind him. She was carrying the large rucksack on her back and, what with her too-large wind-jacket and the other clothing of Jaimie's that she had borrowed, she must have been a very queer sight!

It was when they were about half a mile out of Broadford that the first thing went wrong. The road, which had up to now been merely stony, became positively bumpy, and after a minute or two it was obvious that they had got a puncture.

'It's a good thing we are so near Broadford,' said Angus, wobbling to a standstill and helping Annette to dismount. 'Well, there is certainly no time to stop and mend it now. We shall just have to walk.'

'It will be a nice change,' laughed Annette. 'It was a bit on the cramped side on that step!' Now that they had got started, she was feeling quite cheerful. No mere puncture could depress her. Besides, the rain had creased, and it almost looked as if the sun was coming out.

'There is only one awkward thing about it,' said Angus. 'I had been thinking that perhaps we could continue to ride the bicycle all the way down Glen Arroch to the ferry. The road is being so bad that I do not think a car would manage it after all this rain. However the thing is now settled for us. We must let a lift so far, and do the rest on foot.'

They left the bicycle at a cottage in Broadford, and set off to walk the dozen or so miles that lay between them and the Kylerhea ferry.

'Now for the lift,' said Angus, as several cars, evidently belonging to visitors, passed them. 'I do not agree with thumbing for lifts as a rule, but on this occasion it is, I think, permissible.'

It was easier said than done. Once they had decided to stop a car, the cars ceased to appear, rather as if they had been cut off at the source. Then, when they had almost given up hope, along came a luxurious low-slung American

135

sports convertible. Its driver, a young man in a light suit and broad-brimmed hat, stopped with a screeching of brakes in answer to their frantic signals.

'Hullo!' he exclaimed, leaning out of the door. 'Anything wrong?'

'Could you—I mean, *would* you give us a lift to the Kylerhea road, sir?' asked Angus, running up to the car, his rucksack bumping up and down on his back. (He had taken it from Annette when she dismounted from the bicycle.) 'We're on our way down to the ferry.'

'W-aal, I'm sorry to disappoint you two kids, but there ain't no ferries in this God-forsaken island on Sundays,' drawled the American, having no notion that his speech was contradictory.

Then of course Annette had to explain, and the American became quite interested.

'What d'yer know! You two kids aimin' to walk all that way? Sure, I'll give you a lift. Jump in!'

They shot off along the road to Kyle of Lochalsh and were at the signpost saying KYLERHEA FERRY in two shakes of a duck's tail, as Annette, being country-minded, put it. But now their American friend, generous as all Americans are, wanted to help them still more.

'Say,' he drawled, 'how about driving the old bus' (the glossy sports car) 'along this old road? I take it you kids wouldn't say no to a lift all the way down to the ferry?'

'I should just say not!' exclaimed Annette. 'Oh, you *are* a dear!'

The American had never been called that before. He didn't know many English girls, but if this funny plucky little thing with the big dark eyes was a sample of them, then give him English girls every time. Yes, sir! He handed his heart, figuratively speaking, to Annette over the top of his radiator, a-glitter with chromium-plated fog-lamps, spotlights, badges and mascots.

But alas for the plans of mice and men—and rich Americans! All went well for a mile or so. Then, without warning, the road deteriorated, and from a stony track it became something more like a river bed. The small stones became big stones, and then boulders. They had to get out of the car and lift them out of their path. It was a Skye road at its worst. Even Scottish persistence and American swagger lay down and died before it!

'Sorry, folks, but the old bus won't take it,' panted the American, as they pushed from behind to dislodge the beautiful streamlined car from the deep and muddy ruts. 'And oh, boy, take a look at what's ahead!'

Annette looked; Angus had already done so. A waterfall, that normally splashed down the hillside, across the road and into the ravine opposite in that inconsequent way waterfalls have in the Highlands, had become a roaring torrent, and now their path was barred by a foaming white river. It had washed the road away and made a stony bed for itself several feet deep. One thing was quite clear—the car could go no farther. Indeed, it was a question of how they were going to turn it round and retreat, since there were no side roads, and the 'passing bays', marked by red-painted poles, weren't big enough to allow for reversing. In the end they had to leave the American (cheerful to the last) backing the car all the way to the main road.

'Oh, dear, I feel so guilty!' sighed Annette, as the sound of his going died away. 'But he *would* do it, wouldn't he? I do hope he'll be all right.'

'Och, yes, he will be all right now,' answered Angus. 'And the tale he will be able to tell his friends at home will make up for the discomfort he has suffered. I would have insisted upon going back with him if it would have done any good, though it would have been a dreadful waste of time, and we have none to spare.' He glanced down at his wristwatch. 'It is after twelve o'clock. Come, we must get across this water.' He sat down by the roadside, took off his boots and tied them by their laces round his neck. Then he carried Annette on his back over the torrent. It was so deep that, although his shorts were rolled up to the thighs, they still got wet. Setting Annette down on the far side, he went back for the rucksack.

At the place where the road plunges down the three-mile stretch to the ferry they stopped and ate a couple of sandwiches and a packet of raisins. The precipitous lower slopes of Beinn na Caillich closed in upon them, the same Hill of the Old Woman that Bill, the climber, had pointed out to Annette as they passed through the narrows on the little steamer, *Loch Nevis*, years and years ago—or so it seemed! On their right the ground dropped away to the Kylerhea Glen, a great ravine in the bottom of which a stream thundered with the noise of an express train. It was

137

one of the wildest, grandest places Annette had ever seen. As they sat there a red deer appeared on the top of a crag and stood there, a monarch indeed, sniffing the wind. A great bird floated lazily overhead, so near they could see the jagged wing-tips and the feathers round his legs.

'Yonder is an eagle,' said Angus.

And now they had descended the narrow stony road, as steep in some places as the roof of a house, and were at the ferry. At least they were at the water's edge, but, look as they might, no ferry was to be seen, either on this side of the shore or on the opposite one.

'I have an awful thought,' said Annette. 'I remember Bill—he was my climber friend—saying something about this ferry not operating just now. Not that it matters, of course, because this is Sunday, so long as we can find Dougal and the boat Jaimie told us about.'

They found the ferryman's cottage, but alas, there were no signs of life about it. The door was locked, and, looking through the tiny window, they could see the fireplace black and cold—unthinkable in a Skye dwelling unless it was deserted. Angus began to look anxious indeed. If Annette's Bill was right, and it was highly probable that he was—hikers and climbers usually knew more about the ferries and suchlike than the inhabitants of the island themselves—then Dougal would no longer be living in the little cottage. With a sinking heart Angus made his way round to the tiny boathouse by the shore, which was merely a large and ancient boat turned upside down, with a door added, Annette following close at his heels. It was locked too, but, by putting an eye to a large chink, they could see inside. Then Angus gave a great sigh of relief.

'The boat is there all right.'

'But it's locked,' cried Annette. 'We can't go breaking down the poor man's boathouse.'

'If I am knowing the Skyeman's locks it will not be too difficult,' observed Angus. And this statement proved to be true. After a bit of manipulation the padlock came apart, the crazy door fell open and the boat was theirs. The first part of their journey had come to a successful conclusion. Their escape from the island was assured.

Iт was in this fashion that Annette said farewell to Skye.
Sitting in a tiny rowing-boat with Angus's rucksack at
her feet, and the rain dripping down her neck (yes, it
had begun to rain again by this time), she turned her back
on the depressing sight of Beinn na Caillich, half veiled
by a cloud of rain, and turned to face the great peaks of
the mainland, and particularly Ben Sgriol, which Angus
pointed out as the great mountain round whose flanks they
must pass in order to get to Arnisdale on the shores of
Loch Hourn.

' "Speed bonny boat like a bird on the wing," ' sang
Annette,
"Over the sea from Skye! "

but I'll come back again, never fear. I've loved every
minute of it! '
When they had beached the boat they made their way to
Sandy MacPhee's cottage, following Jaimie's directions,
and, as luck would have it, they found Sandy at home. He
had just returned from 'the kirk at Glenelg', and, at the
mention of Jaimie's name, he led them to a tiny rough
paddock behind the cottage where a sturdy little pony was
grazing.
'I am thinking that the laird is right, and that Shuna is
the best one to help you now,' he said when he had heard
their story, and he led the animal round to the cottage
door, bridled it and put upon its back an ancient leather
saddle. 'But for the moment we will tie her up here, and
you shall come inside and have some tea before you go.'
Angus whispered to Annette that they must accept this
offer. To refuse Sandy's tea would be like throwing his
hospitality in his face and would offend him mortally, and
this they certainly couldn't afford to do since they were
borrowing his pony, if for no other reason. She they went
into the dark little cottage with its earth floor and peat
fire, and found it warm and comfortable. In fact, if they

hadn't been so anxious about the time they would have been only too pleased to stay there indefinitely. On the table, scrubbed to gleaming whiteness, was a fresh baking of scones that Sandy had just made (he was a widower), and he insisted upon giving them an ample supply. 'For ye will be having a long and fearsome journey,' he said, 'round into Loch Hourn and to Arnisdale. The weather is going to be bad. Yes, listen, the wind is rising.'

And so it was! At first they were sheltered by the rising slopes of Meall a' Chaisteil on their left. Then their path dived into the woods, and they could only hear the wind bellowing in the tree-tops, but when they came out into the open, they were met by a positive hurricane of wind and rain. All this time, although, as we know, Annette hated and feared horses, she had ridden Shuna without a word of protest, and indeed her feet were so sore that she was only too glad to be carried along, even on a pony's back. And after riding the patient little Shetland for an hour or so, she began to lose her fear, and even came to look upon Shuna as a friend. At a rather more sheltered part of the road she slipped from the animal's back.

'It's your turn now, Angus,' she said. 'I feel as fit as if I'd had a night's rest.'

At first Angus demurred. 'Think you I can ride myself and let a lassie walk alongside?' he exclaimed. But when Annette pointed out that it was cold sitting still all the time on the pony's back, and that it would warm her up to walk for a bit, he saw her point and mounted Shuna himself. It would be wrong to say he swung himself into the saddle, but rather that he bestrode the little animal, his legs dangling almost to the ground.

And so they went on, slowly, painfully, traversing the miles and miles of wild and mountainous country that lies along the northern shores of Loch Hourn between Glenelg and Arnisdale. If they hadn't been so worried, or if the weather had been finer, they would have been entranced at the beauty of the scenery, but as it was they pushed onwards, their eyes mostly on the ground, because by now the road had become a mere stony track, sometimes almost lost in the boggy wilderness. As they grew more tired they stumbled over the mossy stones and boulders in the path, and if they hadn't been wearing strong boots they might well have sprained or badly bruised their ankles. The little

Sheltie, however, seemed quite tireless and picked her way daintily along the path, avoiding potholes and stones by what must have been instinct, since her eyelashes were encrusted with sleet which was now falling as their path mounted high up the mountain side, and she obviously couldn't see properly where she was going.

They had passed the lonely Loch na Lochain that Jaimie had told them about, and now their path dived into the woods. Sometimes, through gaps in the trees, they caught sight of the loch with the rain clouds sweeping over it, but most of the way the woodland was so thick that they could see nothing but trees, and at times it was almost dark.

The sun was beginning to set when they at last came out of the woods. Annette was riding again now, and by this time the wind had dropped and the setting sun shone with a watery gleam, turning the loch to silver. It began to look less like its name—the Loch of Hell—though not for long. The lower slopes of Ben Sgriol closed in upon the path. Black precipices, glistening with moisture and scored with waterfalls, loomed over them. They found it hard to hear each other speak above the tumult of falling water. And then suddenly the road turned and they saw houses below them, clustered round a bay of white sand.

'Arnisdale!' exclaimed Angus. 'I forgot you came upon it so suddenly.'

'Oh, Angus, Angus!' cried Annette. 'I can't believe it. I was beginning to think that Arnisdale was just a dream, and that we would never come to it at all.'

'That's because you're hungry,' declared Angus. 'Now that we're in sight of it let's stop and eat everything we've got because, although it looks so near, we've still got a good way to go.'

So they had a real feast. With the knowledge that there was no longer any need to save any food, Angus produced a large block of milk chocolate, a packet of biscuits, several oatcakes and a bag of sultanas. They sat down on a wet black rock and ate till they could eat no more. The little pony stood there patiently, waiting their bidding, and suddenly Annette felt a rush of gratitude towards the animal, without whose help they certainly could not have got so far. She flung her arms round its warm neck.

'Darling Shuna!' she said. 'Thank you for carrying me all this way. I'm sorry I said things about horses.'

141

Shuna regarded her mildly. One never knew what these human beings were after. Who but a human would come out on such a day and walk for miles and miles along the side of a loch with not a single blade of decent grass anywhere? It all went to show that human beings were not quite right in the head, and that one must be patient with them.

'We'll have you a horsewoman yet,' teased Angus. 'Following the hounds, I shouldn't wonder!'

'Oh, no I shan't,' retorted Annette with spirit. 'Darling Shuna is one thing and a great vicious horse is entirely another. As for fox-hunting——'

'We all know your views upon *that*!' laughed Angus.

'I've just been thinking,' went on Annette, changing the subject: 'all these kind people who have helped us—Dougal with his boat—although he doesn't know we've borrowed it—Sandy lending us his pony, these people at Arnisdale. Oughtn't we to pay them something?'

'You did not think we ought to pay our American friend for driving us in his car down Glen Arroch,' said Angus.

'Oh, but that was quite different.'

'How was it "quite different"?' asked Angus.

'Well, he was a rich American,' answered Annette. 'You could see that by his car.'

'Although neither Dougal nor Sandy are rich men, nor, I imagine, are the Gordons of Arnisdale, yet they have their pride. Besides, they are friends and kinsmen of Jaimie's, and, unless you wish to offend them, you will not offer to pay them.'

'Well, if you're quite sure——' faltered Annette.

'Of course I am quite sure, *mo chridhe*,' Angus said.

'There you go again—using that word! I do wish you'd tell me what it means.'

'It means that we must be getting on down to Arnisdale,' laughed Angus, pulling her to her feet. 'It is beginning to grow dusk.'

THEY were very tired when they arrived at Arnisdale. Only Shuna seemd as fresh as ever, though even she was glad to see the bucket of oats Fiona Gordon (Andrew Gordon's wife) put in front of her, and a nice warm stable.

'Andrew will be very sorry not to be at home to welcome you,' she said when she heard who they were, and that they were friends of Jaimie's. 'Any friends of Airdrochnish are also friends of ours, we being kin to him.'

'You mean—you mean that Andrew is away from home?' said Angus, dismay sounding in his voice.

'He is awa' to Inverness,' said Fiona, 'wi' Willie MacFarlane.'

'And I suppose he has taken his boat—the motor boat, I mean—with him?' said Angus, while Annette stood there with sinking heart. If Andrew's boat wasn't there, all was lost.

'Och, no, he is awa' i' Willie's boat,' said Andrew's wife cheerfully. Then she saw Angus's troubled face, and guessed what he was thinking.

'You were wanting Andrew to take you across the loch?' she said in her soft voice. 'Och, then there is no reason why you should not be borrowing the boat. Andrew would be wishing you to take her, as he is not here himself to take you across.' She did not ask Angus if he could manage the boat, but took it for granted. Had he not lived in Skye for the best part of his life?

After they had seen Shuna fed and bedded down for the night, they went into the little square stone farmhouse, with its two dormer windows sticking up like ears, and Andrew Gordon's wife gave them of her best. Not that she had a great deal to offer, for visitors were few and far between in this isolated village, and there was no 'little shop' round the corner where you could buy extra provisions. But she put in front of them large plates of stewed mutton, and

143

potatoes cooked in their jackets, and freshly baked oatmeal scones to go with them. Annette and Angus felt that they had never in all their lives eaten such a delicious meal.

While Fiona made the tea, Angus glanced across at Annette and saw that her eyes were closing, and that she was in danger of falling asleep where she sat, and he knew that Jaimie had been right and that they must stop the night here in Arnisdale. For himself, he might have risked crossing the loch that evening, especially as the weather had taken a turn for the better and it was now quite calm (one never knew how long it would last in the Highlands, and he would have liked to complete their journey and have been at Mallaig that night) but, looking at Annette, he knew that she must have slept before they set out on the last lap of their journey.

Fiona took it for granted that they were staying for the night, and, while they ate, she bustled about getting the spare room ready for Annette and a shake-down in the kitchen for Angus.

'We shall have to be up at crack of dawn,' he warned Annette, when they said goodnight. 'No later than five o'clock if we are to be at Mallaig in time to catch the seven forty-two train. We shall have to take care not to sleep in.'

'I am getting up at five o'clock myself most mornings,' Fiona assured them. 'I will call you in plenty of time.'

Before she got into bed, Annette saw across the loch the great mountain Ladhar Bheinn* with a crown of gold upon his head. Although it was almost dark down here, the sun was just touching the tops of the peaks. The waters of Loch Hourn were like dark-blue and green shot silk. She climbed into the old-fashioned four-poster, piled high with a huge feather-bed, and on top an eiderdown made of softest goose feathers, and was asleep almost before her head touched the pillow.

Five minutes later, or so it seemed, she was wakened by a banging on her door and Angus's voice calling her.

'Annette! Get up quickly! It is a quarter to five. We must be away in fifteen minutes.'

Half asleep, Annette dressed and went downstairs to the kitchen. It was flooded with mellow lamplight, for it was not yet fully light, and a lovely smell of fried bacon met

* Pronounced, Lar-ven

her at the door. Angus had already finished his breakfast, and, while Annette ate hers, he went out to see to the boat. As the grandfather clock on the stairs chimed five o'clock he was back again, saying that all was ready. With a parting hug for Fiona, and an assurance that she'd come back again, yes she'd surely come back again, Annette, who was now dressed in her own clothes, went down to the little jetty, where they found most of the inhabitants of the village assembled to see them off—the story of their journey from Airdrochnish had already flown round. And so they said goodbye to Arnisdale, surely one of the most isolated and lonely places in all the Western Highlands, but full of kind hearts for all that.

The weather was fine once more, and they chugged away down the loch on a pathway of silver and rose that the rising sun had laid down upon the still waters of Loch Hourn. So calm was it that not a ripple disturbed the reflections of the mountains on the mirror-like surface of the water. When they got to the mouth of the loch and out into the Sound of Sleat, the boat began to rock gently on the waves, and over the blue water they could see the shores of Skye, and, as they turned towards Mallaig, they could see to the north-east the mountains of Glen Shiel, and out at sea, swimming in a blue haze, the Cuillin of Rhum, shadowy, mysterious.

'I wonder where Bill is?' thought Annette. 'Just starting off to climb one of those peaks, I expect.'

They reached Mallaig in plenty of time to catch the train, and Angus and she stood at the carriage window talking. And so their fearsome journey ended on a quiet note. The only thing Annette regretted was that she'd forgotten to say goodbye to Shuna. And thinking of Shuna brought something else to her mind.

'Oh, Angus—how will you get her back to Sandy?' she asked, suddenly realizing that, although her own journey was ended, and she was safely in the train, Angus had to retrace his own steps.

'That will be easy,' answered Angus. 'When there is no train to catch, and no Annette to look after, I shall be taking the road quietly, and Shuna and I will enjoy ourselves. Not that,' he added hastily, 'I did not enjoy your company, Annette—it was precious indeed—but it was

145

making me a little anxious, not knowing whether we were going to get you here in time.'

But Annette was hardly listening to him. Her ever vivid imagination was picturing to her all the miles and miles of wild country poor Angus had to travel all by himself. Back to Arnisdale in the motor boat, all the way along the stony track round Loch Hourn to Glenelg, across the narrows in Dougal's little boat, up and up precipitous Glen Arroch to Broadford, where nothing but a punctured bicycle awaited him. Even then his journey wasn't ended. He must push the bicycle all the way back to Airdrochan—along the shores of Loch Cill Chriosd, bordered by water-lilies and haunted by water-horses. All that long way because she, Annette, wanted to have the chance of dancing in the mere *corps de ballet* in a film. Oh, she was spoilt—yes, very spoilt!

'Oh, Angus!' she said in an agony. 'All that awful long way!' She hung out of the window. 'Darling Angus— goodbye, Angus!'

'Goodbye, *mo chridhe*,' said Angus gravely.

She had called him her darling, but of course she did not mean it—not the way *he* meant it. He had wanted to kiss her goodbye, but he would not. He had promised her never to offend again.

Being a woman, albeit a very young one, Annette immediately wished that Angus *had* kissed her goodbye. She had hung out of the window and as good as asked him to, but Angus had given her his promise and she knew he wouldn't break it. Yes, she knew that! If there was one person more stubborn than Annette Dancy, that person was Angus Alexander MacCrimmon. No, Annette would have to do the asking herself next time! She sighed. Life was sometimes very difficult.

'Why the sigh?' said a voice at her elbow.

Annette turned round from the corridor window. A stranger stood there, a middle-aged man with hair going grey at the temples, and a small military moustache.

'I was thinking how queer men are,' said Annette.

'Have you known a great many?' asked the stranger politely.

'One or two,' said Annette. 'I was really thinking of Angus—he's the boy who saw me off. He's not a bit like

146

Maximilian, my brother. But of course Max is a dancer, so perhaps that explains it.'

'Oh, so your brother is a dancer?' said the stranger with interest. 'Is he in a ballet company?'

'Oh, goodness no!' exclaimed Annette. 'Max despises ballet. He's a Spanish dancer. It's I who am in the ballet. At least, at the moment I'm in the Cosmopolitan Ballet School, but I hope to be in the Company before long.'

She talked away, telling him all about her dancing-school, the Scottish tour that had ended up at the Skye Gathering Ball, and how she had danced the chief rôle in the ballet, *La Sylphide*. The strange man listened attentively, fascinated by the expressions that passed over her face. She wasn't pretty, no, but she had charm.

'But of course it was just a flash in the pan,' she ended. 'I shall have to go into the backest row of the *corps de ballet* for the rest of my life—well, nearly, anyway. I promised Monsieur Georges I would, without a murmur.'

'Georges Reinholt?' said the stranger.

Annette was struck dumb with surprise for a moment.

'Yes,' she said, when she had recovered. 'Do you know him? Isn't he beautiful?' Her eyes began to shine at the mere thought of her hero.

'Well, I should hardly call him that,' laughed her companion. 'But I know him all right—he is a great friend of mine. As a matter of fact, I had lunch with him not so very long ago.'

'Lunch?' The word broke into Annette's train of thought. She suddenly realised how long ago it was since she had eaten her breakfast in the Arnisdale farm-house, and how very hungry she was. 'I suppose you don't know if one can get anything to eat on this train? Oh, but of course it's still too early for lunch, isn't it? I was forgetting I had my breakfast at five o'clock.'

'I'm afraid there isn't a dining-car on the train,' said the stranger, 'but my hotel put me up a few sandwiches and a flask of coffee which I would very much like to share with you. There are quite enough for two. Could I persuade you?' He motioned to the compartment beside which they both stood, on the seat of which a thermos-flask and a large packet of sandwiches stood invitingly.

Now you might have thought that Mrs Dancy, like most mothers, would have told Annette 'not to talk to strangers,'

147

but you see there *were* no strangers at Mintlaw. Everybody knew everybody. Besides, Annette *always* talked to strangers, always made friends with people wherever she went, so it wouldn't have been any use. But for all that, she was an excellent judge of character. As Bella said, 'Miss Annette has her heed screwed on aal reet, and she'll come to nee harm.' She looked up at the stranger and saw the laughter lines round his mouth and the direct gaze of his grey eyes, and knew that here was someone she could trust. Besides, was he not a friend of her beloved Monsieur Georges? What more need be said?

'Oh, thank you,' she said. 'If you really think you've got plenty.' Together they went into the compartment, and Annette was so busy telling her friend about her escape from Skye on the Sabbath Day that she never noticed it was a first-class one. Nor did she notice her companion slip a ten-shilling note into the ticket-collector's hand when he came to collect the tickets.

Oh, what a lovely meal it was! The hotel hadn't stopped at mere sandwiches. They had risen to sausage-rolls too, and buttered scones, and biscuits and slab cake. There was even cheese to finish off with, and a couple of rosy apples, not to mention the flask of milky coffee.

'You'd think they knew I was going to be here,' said Annette, wiping her mouth on her hankie. 'The dear things! You couldn't possibly have eaten all that yourself, could you? As for me—you've saved my life! I never knew before that five o'clock in the morning was so early! I should have faded away before we got to Fort William. I have a disgustingly healthy appetite—most ballet-dancers have.'

Outside their windows the lovely little stations were gliding past—Arisaig, Beasdale, Lochailort. The Cuillin of Rhum had vanished, the blue sea, the glittering white sands, had been left behind, and Annette hadn't even noticed. Her heart was once more with her dancing. It had flown ahead of her and was already in London—London, where she would be herself, if all went well, this very night. Angus would have said she was like a dragon-fly, hovering over a rushy pool, dancing here, there and everywhere, flying from one place to another, full of the joy of living, never stopping even for a moment to ask what it was all about. But he was wrong in one particular. Often, when

148

she was in bed at night in her tiny room at the top of the Convent Home, Annette would think of these lovely places, and in her dreams she would stand on the top of Blaven and see once more the rocky horseshoe of the Black Cuillin Hills of Skye.

## Dancer's Luck

THEY arrived at Fort William at a quarter to nine and found the sun shining.

'Yes,' said Annette casually, as she looked up at snow-crowned Ben Nevis, 'he's quite a fine mountain, isn't he? But for myself I prefer the Cuillin. I find them a great deal more interesting.' Since she had last trodden Fort William's streets she had seen *real* mountains; she had become a judge of mountains! Her companion didn't answer, but then, thought Annette, perhaps he hadn't seen the Black Cuillin.

They had only a few minutes in which to catch their train to Glasgow. Her companion was catching a plane to London from that city, and Annette (so she told him) was going on to Edinburgh where, with luck, she would get a train to King's Cross which would get her to London just in time for the audition.

'It's to be held on the stage,' she said, 'after the ballet performance in the theatre. Oh, I know it seems late,' she added knowledgeably, 'but these producers are all a little mad, you know, and it wouldn't surprise me if the old boy had decided to hold his audition at three o'clock in the morning.'

'Indeed!' said the stranger with interest.

They travelled third class to Glasgow, and the stranger insisted upon giving Annette luncheon in the restaurant car. As a matter of fact they were both rather glad to escape from their compartment for a bit. Their fellow travellers were a spotty-faced schoolboy who sucked acid drops and read comic papers all the way, and several women who talked about babies and knitting-patterns. Neither Annette nor her companion could get up much enthusiasm for any of them, and, as they hadn't been able to get seats together, they couldn't talk to each other.

In the dining-car it was different. Sitting opposite each other, with the little pink-shaded lamp joggling in between, Annette told the stranger all about Mintlaw, and Sarah's Timmy who had been caught in a gin-trap and lost one of her legs, about Angus and the detested fox-hunting ('but really he's quite a nice boy apart from that'), about the R.A.D. examination, and how she had had to ride through the flood to get to it and had failed to pass after all.

'But Monsieur Georges saw me,' she went on, 'and gave me a place in his school, so it's no wonder I adore him, when he thinks as much of me as all that, is it?'

'No wonder at all,' said the stranger equivocally.

By the time they reached Glasgow the strange man knew Annette's whole life history, even to her French ancestors. He found a seat for her in the general waiting-room, and charged her to stay there until he returned.

'I must go and see about my plane,' he said, 'but when I've done that I shall come back and see what can be arranged for you. Now don't move away from here....'

As we know, Annette never *had* been reasonable in her actions. If she was told to stay in one place, she always wandered away. She didn't mean to—it just happened. While she was sitting there, her eye was caught by the notice-board showing the times of departure of the trains. She would just slip across and see what time the Edinburgh train went, and be back in two shakes of a duck's tail.

No sooner thought of than done! She was standing under the board and running her finger down the list of trains. Ah! Here it was—Dep. Glasgow 2.8. She glanced down at her wrist-watch. The time was now half past twelve, so she had more than an hour to wait. Oh, well—it was better to have too much time than too little. She went back to the waiting-room and sat down again.

Suddenly an awful thought struck her. Half past twelve? Surely that was very early? She had understood from Angus that the journey from Fort William to Glasgow took more than five hours. In a panic she held the watch to her ear. She could hear nothing. Oh, heavens! It couldn't have stopped, it *couldn't*! But it had. In her frantic rush to Mallaig she had forgotten to wind it up. The twelve-thirty was the night before!

'Oh, please, *please* could you tell me the time?' she begged, rushing over to a bald-headed man who was sitting reading a newspaper at a table. 'Quickly, quickly, please!'

'The time?' Slowly he took a large turnip-watch out of his waistcoat pocket and snicked it open. 'Let me see—I'm a little slow, I believe, but it must be about two o'clock. No, perhaps, five minutes past. As I say, I'm a trifle slow.'

'Oh, no!' cried Annette. 'Oh, no! It can't be!'

She dashed out of the waiting-room, quite forgetting that she was supposed to stay there, and leaving the bald-headed man staring.

'What an extraordinary child!'...

Meanwhile Annette had reached the barrier to Platform Four, from which, according to the notice-board, the Edinburgh train was due to depart in exactly three minutes.

'The two-eight train to Edinburgh?' she gasped.

'It's just awa',' said the ticket-collector cheerfully. 'Hurry, lassie, ye'll catch it mebbie, if ye run. Hi, wait a minute! I havna got your ticket.'

Annette skidded to a standstill.

Her ticket? Where was it? In the pocket of her mackintosh, of course. But it wasn't there. Nor was it in the pocket of her skirt. In short, it wasn't anywhere.

'I've got my ticket,' she told the man. 'I have, really. I had it just a minute ago when I got out of the Fort William train. Please, *please* let me through. You don't know how important it is. Honestly, it's life or death.'

'Maybe it is, and maybe it isn't,' returned the man. 'But I'll no' can let ye through without a ticket. You be quick and find it, lassie, or ye'll miss yon train. . . . In fact, ye've missed it noo!'

It was only too true! Slowly the long train drew out of the station, while Annette, from the other side of the barrier, watched it in horror. Yes, as she stood there, the red lights on its tail slowly but irrevocably disappeared from view. It was like being in a nightmare!

And then the awfulness of her situation struck Annette like a blow. All that long, long weary journey, overcoming what seemed like impossible obstacles, and then to lose her train just because her watch had stopped and she couldn't find her ticket! It was too much for her! Before the horrified eyes of the ticket-collector, and a group of interested people who didn't want to miss anything, she crumpled up gently and fell in a dead faint at their feet.

When she came to her senses she was lying on a couch in the station-master's office, and her friend of the train was bending over her.

'Where am I? What happened? ... Oh, it's you again!'

'I thought I told you to stay in the waiting-room, young woman?' said the man severely. 'Yes, it's me again, and it's rather a good thing you made such a stir by fainting away, so that I had no difficulty in finding you. I think I may be able to help you.'

'Nobody can help me now!' cried Annette wildly, remembering what had happened, 'It's gone—the train, I mean. The only train that would have got me to Edinburgh in time to get to London this evening.'

'Och, lassie,' put in the station-master, 'yon train would-na hae got ye to Edinburgh in time for the evening train to London. It doesna get there till three-nine, and the only train to get ye to London this evening is awa' lang before that, so it's just as well ye didna catch it.'

Poor Annette didn't know what to say to this. If what he said was true, then it *was* just as well. Still, here she was still in Glasgow, and it certainly looked as if she wasn't going to be able to get to London tonight after all. Her tears began to fall again. For the past twenty-four hours excitement had kept her going, but now reaction had begun to set in, and she knew how deadly tired she was.

'My audition—my audition——' was all she could say.

'Your audition does not matter,' said the strange man. 'Believe me, it does not matter one jot.'

Not matter? Believe him? Once again Annette sighed at the stupidity of the non-professional person. Not matter, indeed! That's all *he* knew!

'But if you are quite determined to get to this audition,' he was saying, 'you shall accompany me on my plane. Now it is quite all right'—he cut short her expostulations—'I know quite well that you have no spare money, but, on the other hand, I have a spare seat to offer you which will be going begging if you do not accept it.'

Annette began to be aware that there was an authorita-tive 'something' about this stranger. He was the sort of per-son who waved magic wands and got what he wanted. She gave a sigh of relief and laid her burden, figuratively speaking, upon his shoulders.

'Thank you,' she said, 'I'll come with you.'

A car was waiting for them at London Airport, so they were in the City soon after six. Annette's friend put her down on the steps of her Convent Home and said goodbye.

'At least let us make it *au revoir*,' he amended. 'Since we have a mutual friend in our Monsieur Georges, it is quite possible that we shall meet in the not too distant future.'

'Oh, I do hope so,' said Annette. 'You just don't know what you've done for me. You've saved everything. Even if I don't get into the *corps*, at least I shall have had a shot at it. Goodbye, Mr—oh, I don't believe I even know your name.' She ran after the taxi.

'Goldberg,' said the man at the window.

'Goodbye, Mr Goldberg! I shall never, never forget you!'

She went into the Home, and, as supper wasn't until seven, she went to her room to wait for it. Her heart was so light that she had never even thought about the many flights of stairs she had to climb to get to it. She sat down in the window-seat, and a ray of the setting sun fell upon her upturned face. Oh, it was lovely to be back again, even if the view wasn't to be compared with that from her window at Airdrochan Castle.

The clocks in their clock-towers all around began chiming the half-hour. A flock of pigeons rose with a clatter of wings from the church steeple across the way and settled on the roof-top. One of them came and perched on Annette's window-sill. She laughed aloud. He looked so pompous and important—just like the business-man who had told her the time in the waiting-room in Glasgow station!

She went down to supper, then came back to her room, washed, did her hair, put on her dressing-gown and then lay down upon her hard little bed to rest until it was time for her to go. She set her alarm-clock and made sure she had really wound it up this time. No more slips, thought Annette with a shudder! At half past nine she put on a rather less crumpled skirt, and a clean blouse which had two buttons missing, then took up a large cardboard box containing a spotless and creaseless white *tutu*, tucked a

153

pair of nicely broken-in point-shoes under her arm, and was ready to face the world. No-one would have imagined that this was the selfsame weary overwrought girl who had fainted in the middle of Glasgow station, and in this Annette showed the true temperament and stamina of the ballet-dancer.

When she arrived at Beaufort Street, off Oxford Circus, people were pouring out of the Cosmopolitan Theatre, so she knew that the performance was just over. Up and up the six flights of stairs she went to the students' dressing-rooms.

They were all there—Paddy, Rita, Marie and even Simonetta—getting into their *tutus*, making up their faces. It was just as if she had never been away.

'Oh, hullo, Annette! Sure an' I thought you weren't going to make it!' cried Paddy. 'Be quick now, mavourneen! We've to be down in ten minutes. The Great Man is here already!'

'Shan't be a minute,' cried Annette, undressing at lightning speed. She had got her *tutu* on, and was just putting her hair in a net when the door opened and Kevin, one of the call-boys, put his head round it.

'Annette Dancy, you're wanted on stage.'

'Me?' cried Annette, looking round under her arm. 'Are you sure it's me they want?'

'Sure!' grinned the boy. He went off down the stairs, and they could hear him calling, 'Annette Dancy wanted on stage . . . Annette Dancy wanted on stage . . . Annette Dancy . . .', the call getting fainter and fainter as Kevin descended.

'I think our Kevin likes Annette's name!' laughed Rita, but Paddy said afterwards that Kevin, being Irish like herself, had the gift of second-sight, and was getting into practice!

Away went Annette along the dusty galleries, down the echoing stairs, past the empty dressing-rooms, to the darkened theatre, which only a short time ago had been full of light and laughter. And so to the stage. Monsieur Georges was there, talking to the Great Man, who had his back towards her.

'*Venez ici, mon enfant!*' said Monsieur Georges. 'Come here, Annette, my child. I have here someone to see you.'

It was at this moment that the Great Man turned round,

and he wasn't a Great Man at all! He was—oh, no, impossible! Quite impossible! There was clearly come mistake.

'Hullo, Annette!' said her friend of the train.

'This,' said Monsieur Georges, 'is Mr Stanley Goldberg, who is going to choose the cast for the ballet *La Sylphide* in his film. He tells me you have met before.'

'But—but——' gasped Annette.

'Wait!' ordered Monsieur Georges with a dramatic gesture, that Annette, had she not been so overcome, would have been the first to appreciate. "Annette, *chérie*, your friend here, who, as he has no doubt told you, is *my* friend too, insists that you dance the rôle of La Sylphide in his film. As for me I am all disapproval. It should be work, work, work for you, *mon enfant*. But who am I to refuse the so earnest request of my friend? *Eh bien*, Annette? What do you say?'

Now Annette was full of guile. She knew (who better?) that her Monsieur Georges loved the dramatic. He liked to think of himself as a dictator—a Petipa, a Vestris, a Cecchetti, or perhaps a Taglioni (*père*), using his dancers as his tools. He, Monsieur Georges, deciding their fates and fortunes! Annette knew this. She swept him a low curtsy, right down to the ground; and remained there at his feet.

'It is not what *I* wish, but what *you* wish, *mon maître*,' she said humbly.

'*Ah ça!*' exclaimed Monsieur Georges. 'Get up, get up, my child! Who am I to stop you? But after zis film——'

'It is work, work, work! Yes, *mon maître*, I promise,' said Annette meekly.

# Letters

THE next evening, after she had got back from the first rehearsal of *La Sylphide*, which had been, of course, at the film studio, Annette sat in her window-seat writing to Deborah. The first part of her letter, which was all about her adventurous dash to Mallaig, doesn't concern us, for we know it already, but I think we might look over her shoulder and read the last part:

*This is really the end of the story. You see, Mr Gold-berg (the kind gentleman I met on the train) was the director of the film, and he was on that yacht that was riding at anchor in Portree harbour the night of the Skye Gathering Ball. He actually saw me dance, only he thought I was Simonetta. He was coming all the way to London to sign up Simonetta for his film, and then he met me in the train and found out everything, and if that isn't my dancer's luck, I don't know what is! The strange thing is that there we both were in Skye together, and I need never have made my terrific dash away from you all, and he needn't have dashed to London either, and yet if we hadn't both done it we wouldn't have met, and he'd have gone on thinking I was Simonetta to the end of his life.*

*Poor Simonetta—I feel very sorry for her, though she is my deadly rival. She's always wanted to be in a film. However, she's been accepted for Sadler's Wells at the New Year, so I expect she'll get over it.*

*Oh, and I simply must tell you—I've been airborne (I think that's what they call it) for the very first time. Yes, Mr Goldberg let me have a spare seat on the plane from Glasgow. What a thrill! As a matter of fact it was a very small plane and there were only two seats in it. Do you think it could have been specially chartered? I love to think so! I do think it was too bad of Mr G. to keep me guessing like that, don't you? But, as he said, he had to speak to Monsieur Georges before he told me.*

*Well, now I've come to the end of my letter, and all that remains is to tell you how sorry I was to have to leave you all like that. It wasn't that I wasn't having the loveliest time ever, but because of my dancing. You do understand, dearest Deborah, don't you? I shall remember you always and always. And, of course, dear Blaven, and Airdrochan Castle, and everything.*

*With lots and lots of love,*
*Annette.*

*P.S. When I picked my mac up off the floor tonight I heard a jingling sound, and found that all my spare money (the two and fourpence-ha'penny I had left after*

*buying my ticket) had slipped through a hole in my
pocket. While fishing it out I found an india-rubber, two
hair-nets, a piece of toffee and—my lost ticket!!* **P.P.S.**
*If you really do come to London on your way back to
America, do* please *let me know, because I should like
to give you all a hug.*

Love again, Annette.

As an author I realise how much readers dislike 'loose
ends', so I expect you all want to know—like Annette—
what happened to Poppa and his fish, and also what Sheena
said when she found old Seumas's bicycle missing, so I
think I had better let you read Deborah's letter in answer
to Annette's. Here it is then:

Castle Airdrochan,
Isle of Skye

*Darling Annette,*
  *Thank you a whole lot for your letter and all your
news. We were all thrilled to the back teeth about your
success. Not that we were surprised, mind you. You sure
deserve it, honey—you've got plenty of guts! Fancy you
meeting the great Stanley Goldberg on the train. That
sure was a whole great big slice of luck!*
  *Now for some red-hot news of our own. What d'you
know! Jaimie has broken out into films! Yes, the same
film as you, and in fact he's got the name part. They
are calling the film 'Cock o' the North', and they were
scouting round to find someone romantic-looking to play
it. He had to be able to climb mountains, and do Highland dancing, and talk with a Scottish accent, so you
can guess they weren't finding it all that easy. Then Mr
Dagleish, the film producer (the opposite number to your
Mr Goldberg) saw Jaimie at the 'ceilidh', and he knew
straight away that he'd found his man. And would you
believe it, the laird said nothing to anybody, and none
of us knew a thing, until Mr Dagleish turned up at the
castle and spilled the beans. You sure do have some
dark horses over here! Angus says that Jaimie isn't
going to turn film star—in fact he hates the very idea
of acting in films, but he's steeled himself to make just
this one film and by so doing retrieve the family for-*

tunes. He'll make enough money on this one film to be able to go on living in Skye, and to keep Airdrochan Castle and the village as they ought to be kept. I think he's really an awful nice young man, even if he is a dark horse. Sheena has just come in, and she says he's not as nice as I imagine, but I think she's mistaken, don't you?

And oh, honey—talking of Sheena, the most awful thing happened to her. You know she was to have an audition for a Scottish dancing team that was going over to Canada? Well it was to be on the day after you left—the Monday. Of course there was no transport, as Pop had the automobile, so she'd arranged with Seumas for the loan of his bicycle to get her to Broadford where she could catch a bus to Portree. Well, off she went on the Monday morning, and when she got to Strathbeg—no bicycle! Angus and you had borrowed it, not knowing, of course, that she wanted it. Seumas said that the laird had told him to lend it to the lassie (you, Annette), and as far as he, Seumas, was concerned, that was that, the laird being his foster-brother! (You know what these Highlanders are about their kinship and things!) Of course Jaimie hadn't the slightest idea that he was spoiling Sheena's chances. The poor darling would have been devastated if he'd known that, when she eventually got to Portree, the audition was over long ago, the team chosen, and the judges half way back to Mallaig in the steamer!

Well! I really think I've told you most everything.
All our love, Deb.

P.S. Gosh! I nearly forgot to tell you about Poppa. A basket of fish arrived today, but no address, and nothing to say when he is coming back. Can you beat it? Momma's getting real fond of walking. I shall get her up to the top of Blaven yet!
Love once more, D.

*Author's Note.* And if you are inclined to agree with Sheena in her views about the laird of Airdrochnish, remember that Sheena herself had tried to spoil Annette's chances, and had only been 'hoist with her own petard', or, to put it another way, paid back in her own coin. Also, that with her wild and somewhat unscrupulous nature, she respected Jaimie all the more for what he had done. As she walked up to Coire Uaigneich on the Wednesday after Annette had gone back to London, she sang under her breath:

> 'A Gordon for me! A Gordon for me!
> If you're no a Gordon, you're no use to me!'

And Jamie, coming down the corrie, knew that before the year was out he would be in a position to ask Sheena Mac-Donald to marry him—if he so wished. But it is no use your asking me whether he wished or no, for it would take more than a mere author to read the heart of Jaimie Gordon!

THE END

# ARMADA BOOKS

Hundreds of thousands of boys and girls are collecting our wonderful Armada books. At half-a-crown each, Armada books are magnificent entertainment and value. *Always ask your parents and relatives to buy Armada books for your presents.* Just think, you can have four delightful books for only 10s., eight for one pound! Tell your friends about them. Always ask your newsagent or bookseller for Armada books, but if you have difficulty they may be obtained, price 2s. 10d. each (including postage) from Armada Books, Dorset House, 13a Old Burlington Street, London, W.1.